HEAD TRIP

By the Author

On Dangerous Ground

Head Trip

HEAD TRIP

by

D.L. Line

2010

HEAD TRIP

ISBN 10: 1-60282-187-9
ISBN 13: 978-1-60282-187-3

THIS TRADE PAPERBACK ORIGINAL IS PUBLISHED BY
BOLD STROKES BOOKS, INC.
P.O. BOX 249
VALLEY FALLS, NY 12185

FIRST EDITION: NOVEMBER 2010

CREDITS
EDITOR: CINDY CRESAP
PRODUCTION DESIGN: STACIA SEAMAN
COVER DESIGN BY SHERI (GRAPHICARTIST2020@HOTMAIL.COM)

Acknowledgments

To my mom and dad, for always being supportive, especially in letting me take care of you.

To my brother, Tom, just for being an awesome guy. Thanks for your hard work and all of your attempts to help me get my work out into the world.

To Christina, for everything. And everything else. I just don't know where to start sometimes.

To Emma, Matthew, and Adam, for thinking that this writing thing makes me cool beyond cool. I can always use the help.

To my friends in Virginia and Ohio and wherever else we might find one another. My life is complicated, but your assistance and camaraderie make things so much better. If I start naming names, I'm sure to miss someone, so suffice it to say, you all know who you are.

To my friend, Deb Serrins, for planting the idea for this story in my head and then offering me the chance to run with it. I hope you're pleased with the final product. I could gush about you for hours, but I think we'd better just skip it.

Finally, to the peeps at Bold Strokes Books, especially Cindy Cresap and her skilled editorial hand. Also, to Stacia Seaman for her excellent proofing and Sheri Halal for the cool cover art. Thanks a bunch!

Dedication

This story is dedicated to Christina.
It couldn't have happened without you, but you know this better than anyone. Thank you.

Chapter One

S helby. Earth to Shelby Hutchinson."

Shelby had been daydreaming again, staring at eight years' worth of perfect attendance plaques on her office wall.

"What, Jake? Did you need something?"

"Yeah, it's five o'clock. Time to go." Jake looked impatient while he checked his watch and hiked his computer bag on his shoulder. "Don't forget that the hospital said they weren't going to pay you any more overtime, even if you are the Information Director."

Through the fog of her own fatigue, Shelby remembered that. "Right." She rubbed at her eyes, sore from another in a long string of days staring at her computer screen. "Did you take care of the immunization database for Employee Health?"

"Yes."

"What about Billing? Did you manage to get them back into Patient History?"

"Yes, Shelby, I did. I even reminded them to make sure the system was plugged in, just like you told me to." Jake checked his watch again. "We need to go. C'mon. We've got to get moving. The train is always backed up this time of day." She must have looked confused, so Jake filled in. "Remember we're going to raid that Soviet munitions dump at nineteen hundred."

The game. "Oh, shit. That's right." Shelby jumped out of her chair and began to pack up her own computer bag. "You know, Jake, I'm beginning to think it's a huge problem that I can barely drag my ass through a normal eight-hour day, but as soon as you mention video game adventures and digital munitions dumps, I—"

"Yeah, I get that, but we can talk later. Besides, I had something important I wanted to discuss." He checked his watch for a third time and even pointed at it for emphasis. "Time to go. Badass commies await." He held the door while Shelby shrugged into her long wool coat, but she could tell he had another question.

"Is there something else, Jake?"

"Well, yeah. Did you remember to call that new gal, you know the one from Human Resources?"

"Oh, shit," Shelby muttered softly, "Jake, she's nice, but…"

"But what, Shel?"

She looked away, hesitant to make eye contact. "Well, we kind of were supposed to have a date, but I pretty much bailed on her."

"Shel…" She could hear the exasperation in his voice. "You have to do something besides work, you know?"

"Why, Jake? What difference does it make?"

"Why is because you never take a break. You look tired. You haven't taken a vacation in the four years I've been here. You beg off dates, you blow me off if I try to set up something after work, unless, of course, it's any opportunity to goof around with your PlayStation Thirty-three—"

"You know it's a PS9, and the technology is amazing. Consider it research for work."

"I'll consider it research only if you convince me you've found a way to travel back in time. You know shooting Russian spies went out when the Berlin Wall came down in 1989. That was sixty years ago. I think you need to stop living in the past, and quite frankly, you need to get laid."

Jake was right, but now was hardly the time for that kind of discussion. "Jake, old buddy, I think you can probably find something more interesting to worry about than my sex life. At least I hope you can."

"Well, I do have something else for you, but it can wait until after gaming tonight."

"Okey dokey." As much as she hated to admit it, Jake was right, especially about the getting laid part, but she wasn't particularly interested in a casual relationship, and her own unwillingness to step out of her firmly established comfort zone ruled out everything else. It would happen when it did, and until then...well, until then there were plenty of Russian spies to shoot at on her PlayStation. That was good enough for now.

Shelby nearly tripped as she stepped out of the warm comfort of Northwestern Memorial Hospital and onto the street, pulling her woolly green scarf tighter around her neck against the stiff breeze that seemed to blow in constantly from Lake Michigan. As she pulled her coat closer around her, she began to question the wisdom of her latest short haircut, especially considering the cold reality of Chicago in January. She missed the long hair around the back of her neck, but the scarf did offer some protection.

"Should have worn your hat, doofus," Shelby mused quietly as she ran her gloved fingers through her hair.

"Did you forget it again?"

Shelby didn't even realize she had been talking loudly enough for Jake to hear. "Yeah, I did. No worries."

Habit carried Shelby down the street and up the steps to the train platform, Jake trailing behind just as they did every Wednesday night. She frowned when she thought the little details of her life had become mundane enough that Jake even noticed she'd forgotten her hat again. As the train doors closed behind her, she grabbed the back of her coat to prevent it being caught in the door and closed her eyes against the claustrophobia that threatened to drown her amongst the tight throng of afternoon commuters. She hated the train this time of day.

❖

Shelby tossed her game controller onto the coffee table and yanked off her headset, disgusted by the failure of her team to take the Soviet munitions dump. Actually, it was failure number four of the evening, but who was counting?

"No worries, Shel. We'll take a break and get it the next time." Jake got up from Shelby's tattered recliner and headed toward the refrigerator.

"Yeah, probably," Shelby said. Jake always liked to look at the bright side of things, a fact that made him a great friend but somewhat annoying at the same time. "Thanks." She accepted the frosty bottle Jake had brought from the kitchen. Shelby thought for a moment about declining another drink, but she was already two beers in, and the dark, foamy Guinness was beginning to work its magic on her resolve to make tonight an early evening.

"So, Jake, this morning you said you had something you wanted to talk about. What's up?"

"This." Jake fished around the pockets of his corduroy pants, finally managing to produce a rather wrinkled brochure. "I think you need to look at this."

She took the paper from his hands, debating whether she should be scared more because it was something Jake had come up with or because it was an old-style brochure printed on shiny paper. In this day of advanced technology and supercomputers, Shelby thought things like this had gone the way of the brontosaurus, but here it was. How quaint.

"What the hell, Jake? Head Trip Travel Services? Trendy high-tech vacations for the über-affluent?" She snorted with disgust and tossed the brochure on the coffee table.

"And also, my friend, the answer to your vacation woes."

"Oh no. Are you nuts? I can't take a vacation now. The new system is coming in next week, and we still have the end-of-year stuff to do with Accounting. No, Jake, I can't."

"But, Shel...here. Just look at it. It says you can take a vacation, but they've updated the technology so you can go anywhere without ever leaving the comfort of their office downtown."

As she tentatively opened the folded paper, Shelby wrinkled her nose, unsure of what Jake wanted her to see. "What do you mean?"

"Okay, here's the way I understand it. You go to this place and they do some kind of digital mapping of your brain. Then, based on those results and the other stuff you tell them you want, they make the vacation happen in your head. It's like that thing you did last year when you went to the IS conference in Paris. You remember how you went to that language place and they just imprinted the ability to speak French in your head. That was cool."

"Yeah, that was very cool. It was like a memory, something that I always knew."

"Right," Jake said, "and you don't need to take a whole week off work to get a seven-day vacation. That's the best part. They just strap you in, give you a pill or a shot or something, and you get to spend seven glorious days on a sunny beach full of semi-naked women, but it only takes a couple of hours in real time."

She thought for a moment while she turned the brochure over to look at the back of it. "That sounds okay. But how much…oh, Jesus, Jake. This is expensive."

"Oh, come on, Shel. I know you have the money. Look around your apartment. You live like a college student, despite the fact you have a six-figure income. Every stick of furniture in here is other people's used shit from Craigslist. You never go anywhere, so I'd be willing to bet you've probably squirreled away every dime you've ever made."

"Yeah, I suppose you're right."

"You suppose I'm right?" Jake looked incredulous. "You know I'm right, and you know you need the break. This way you can have all the fun and adventure you want, and you can do it Saturday afternoon. Then, when the new servers come in next week, you'll be all rested and refreshed, and I hope, happily laid."

"I don't know…" Shelby continued to stare at the brochure.

"Wait, here's the best part. You're not limited to locations or time frame. If you want to take a vacation and go shoot Russian spies in 1985, you can do that too."

"Russian spies in 1985? Just like on my PlayStation?" Shelby was interested now. "I could do that. Might be fun."

"See, there you go. Besides, I'm sure you could use a change of pace. You always do the right thing, you're reliable as hell, and a week off to be totally irresponsible in the safety of an office in downtown Chicago sounds exactly like something you need."

"Reliable." Shelby picked at the label of her beer. She had always been reliable. Good old reliable Shelby Hutchinson. Always did the right thing for everyone else. Maybe Jake was right about this.

"Okay. I'll check it out, but no promises."

Jake smiled the smile of temporary victory.

"I'll research this online when we're done here. I need to make sure it's safe and all that."

"I'd expect nothing less."

"Right, because I'm reliable."

"Well, yeah, but I didn't mean that's a bad thing."

"No, of course you didn't." Despite her vocalized agreement, Shelby didn't like that the first thing anyone seemed to think about her was that she was reliable. In her mind, reliable equaled boring, and she didn't want to think of herself as boring. Besides, Russian spies in 1985? That sounded like fun.

❖

Several hours later, Shelby was still staring at the computer screen. The Head Trip Web site taunted her, offering her the opportunity to go anywhere, do anything, and best of all, be anything she wanted.

Despite the fact it was late and she needed to be at work early, Shelby couldn't turn off the computer. Once intrigued, she stayed intrigued, and it only got worse when she began to understand the process. The first step was a short visit to the office for something the company called "digital mapping," a procedure in which they would run her through a series of simulations to gauge her reaction, testing her likes and dislikes. The Web site explained she would be introduced to a number of situations to determine what kind of situation she was attracted to and, as the scenario unfolded, the computer would create Shelby's ideal match based only upon her reactions. If her eyes were drawn to a beautiful brunette, the blondes in the room would fade out. If she preferred her women to have blue eyes, the others would fade as well. This would continue until the computer had enough details to create exactly what Shelby wanted to see and interact with. The process would do the same for everything Shelby wanted in her trip, from the kind of car she wanted to drive to the weather she would experience on the trip. The coolest part was that the vacation didn't actually happen in real time, as they did on the holodeck from the old episodes of *Star Trek* Shelby loved so much. It was more like an implanted memory, except Shelby didn't need to take the vacation in order to have the memory. Head Trip just made it happen. Presto!

Shelby figured she should probably do some of her own research as well. She knew all about 1985 as it was presented in her favorite video game, but a better knowledge of the styles and trends of the time might make the trip more fun. She didn't want to stick out like a sore thumb by wearing the wrong kind of shoes or some weird floppy hat if no one else did. She wanted to be an adventurer, not a spaz. She could do that anytime.

Maybe she could do the digital mapping thing tomorrow on her lunch hour. It was expensive, but Jake had been right about the years of income she had managed to squirrel away. She could definitely afford it, and maybe she owed it to him and the rest of her coworkers to take a real break. She was tired, and she was sure it was beginning to show in the quality of her work. She was not thrilled with the idea of stripping down to her birthday suit for a full body scan, but that was the only way the computer could get authentic, down-to-the-last-freckle kind of detail that would make the experience as lifelike as possible.

"Well, no guts, no glory," she muttered into the air of her sparsely furnished apartment. It only took one touch of a key on her computer to open the digital video link to the company. Smiling nervously, she waited until a young man with blond hair that stood straight up answered her call.

"Hello and welcome to Head Trip Travel Services. My name is Andrew. Where would you like to go today?"

Chapter Two

S helby stood on the platform waiting for the train to transport her from Frankfurt to West Berlin. She was still a little disoriented from the office procedure in frozen downtown Chicago that had left her standing on a rail platform, April sun high in the sky, somewhere in the place still known as West Germany. It was funny how the whole thing worked.

First thing Saturday morning, she had climbed into what could only be described as a technological marvel of a recliner, taken the pill a technician named Lois had given her, slipped the virtual reality helmet over her head, and basically fallen asleep. Her personal research coupled with the propaganda from the company served as proof enough she would be safe and cared for during her day in the office. The fact that she was now standing on a rail platform somewhere in Northern Europe, wearing the tightest pair of jeans she had ever squeezed her butt into, served as ample reminder she was definitely not experiencing the Chicago of the mid twenty-first century.

"This is so cool." Shelby bounced lightly on the balls of her feet. She held one foot out to look at the shoes that were now part of her attire. Cute little white leather high-top sneakers, complete with a double set of Velcro fasteners around the ankles. Those struck her as a great idea, especially considering the button-fly jeans she was now wearing were so tight she wasn't sure if she could manage to bend over to tie the shoes. Oh well, she knew the style was right for 1985, and she would deal with the shoelace problem tomorrow. Shelby liked the bright purple sweatshirt with the hood and the big pocket in the front. She especially liked the old-style logo for her alma mater, Northwestern University, emblazoned all over the front. She reached under the purple fleece to check what else she had been dressed in and discovered quickly that the ribbed knit fabric of her white tank top was no different from the ones currently in her dresser drawer back in Chicago.

"Back in Chicago…" It was weird to think about since she was in reality still in Chicago, but everything she could see, feel, and hear told her it was 1985 and she was in Frankfurt. Her stomach rumbled when the smell of grilled sausages from a street vendor's cart reached her nose. As she ran her fingers through her short hair, she came away relieved that her actual appearance hadn't changed. While her own background research had shown her a style known as "mall hair," she was abundantly grateful she wouldn't have to deal with anything quite so ridiculous. A blow dryer and a comb were all she would need, items she assumed were packed in the black canvas duffel bag sitting next to her feet on the rail platform.

A voice from a loudspeaker overhead announced the imminent arrival of the train to take her to West Berlin. She managed to pick up some of what the male voice had said, but fluency in German was evidently not considered vital to her adventure, so therefore not included. As she looked around the platform, people began milling about, checking their luggage, making their preparations to get on the train. There were a few other young people dressed much like she was, leading her to believe they were American college students, just like she was supposed to be. She contemplated walking up to them and asking how the heck she was supposed to get these pants buttoned again if she needed to go to the bathroom, but decided they would probably think she was crazy and most likely ignore her.

Shelby stopped watching people fiddle with their luggage and kiss loved ones good-bye when she caught sight of a woman who nearly stole her breath away. She stood several yards to Shelby's right, dressed in tight black jeans that hugged her oh-so-shapely behind in a way that Shelby just couldn't stop staring at. "Wow," she breathed out quietly. She let her gaze drift up, over the back of the black leather jacket the woman was wearing. Hair the color of Hershey's milk chocolate tied in a ponytail fell past the collar of the jacket. As if the woman could feel Shelby's eyes freely roaming up and down, she pulled off her mirrored sunglasses and turned to look at Shelby, studying her with the iciest crystal blue eyes Shelby had ever seen. This woman, this Amazon goddess, was breathtaking, and Shelby didn't even bother to try to hide the fact she was staring. The woman returned Shelby's look with a little smile, put her sunglasses back on, and turned her attention toward the train now pulling into the station.

Shelby reached into the large pocket on the front of her sweatshirt and found several items, including a wallet, complete with several hundred Deutschmarks in cash, an Illinois driver's license, and a Visa card. Further examination revealed a United States passport and tickets for the train. She checked the ticket to determine where she needed to sit and stepped back a short distance from the edge of the platform as the train hissed and rattled its way to a stop. Shelby leaned over, as much as the damn tight jeans would allow, picked up her duffel bag, and began to make her way toward the train. Strangely enough, one last look around the platform revealed no trace of Shelby's Amazon with the black leather jacket, but she could worry about that later. She was certain there was adventure on the way, and she was eager to get to West Berlin.

Once aboard, she found her seat, heaved her surprisingly heavy duffel into the overhead compartment, and slid into her seat next to the window. In 1985, there was no such thing as an iPod to listen to, and even if there had been, Shelby was not terribly enamored of the pop/rock nonsense that seemed to be the preferred music of the day. She debated a quick check through her duffel to see if the kind folks at Head Trip had packed her a book, but when she got out of her seat, she spotted her Amazon, sitting alone in a seat at the rear of the car. The mystery woman was staring right at her, her gaze piercing in a way that made Shelby wonder if she actually had X-ray vision. She dismissed the thought quickly. "Yeah, right, genius. A hot babe like that undressing you with her eyes? Sure." Shelby returned the stare with one of her own. The woman averted her eyes to look out the window of the train as it began to move.

Unprepared for the sudden motion of the train, Shelby had to grab the overhead bin to keep from falling. That was certainly no way to impress anyone, much less this vision in black leather Shelby caught staring at her again. What was she looking at? Shelby was puzzled, but decided it would be best to just sit and contemplate the leather-jacketed bombshell from the safety of her seat next to the window. "Well, maybe one last peek." She sat up higher and craned her neck to see over the seat across from her. Shelby stopped, surprised because the Amazon was no longer in her seat. Before she could even take the time to look for her again, the woman appeared, standing in the aisle adjacent to Shelby's seat. Shelby looked up and met the woman's gaze head on as she asked a silent question, raising her eyebrows and pointing toward the unoccupied seat directly across from Shelby.

Shelby nodded and gestured toward the vacant seat, which the woman slid into. While she was hoping for an introduction, or maybe just a small, "Hi, how's the weather, and you're really cute," Shelby got nothing. Rather than try to make conversation, the woman pulled headphones from the pocket of her jacket and put them on. She reached back into her pocket, started some kind of music player, slipped on her sunglasses, and turned to look out the window. As she let her own fantasies about hot babes on trains drift away, Shelby settled back into her seat, gave in to the motion of the train, and fell asleep.

Shelby awoke with a stretch and a yawn as a conductor wove

his way down the aisle announcing the train's arrival in West Berlin. She was still a little disoriented and quickly noticed her fantasy Amazon was once again missing. Although she wasn't completely sure why, Shelby knew she was supposed to get off the train in West Berlin and make her way toward the Meininger City Hostel on Meininger Strasse. She had actually allowed Andrew, the guy from Head Trip, to explain that much before she stopped him, telling him her friends thought she was boring, and she had something to prove to herself. She would play this trip from the seat of her pants and hope for the best. Besides, it was only a computer simulation, and who knew computers better than she did? Andrew had seemed reluctant, but she turned on her best smile and charmed him into acquiescence.

As she struggled to get her black duffel from the overhead bin, Shelby caught sight of her mystery woman through the window. Still wearing her mirrored sunglasses, she was already on the platform, and it looked to Shelby like she was waiting for someone. Since Shelby had no choice but to be patient while the passengers clogging the aisle of the train removed their own belongings from the overhead bins, she never took her eyes off the woman. Once the people began to move, Shelby continued her study, noticing how the woman looked over first one shoulder, then the other. She checked her watch, she shifted her weight from one black booted foot to the other, she took her sunglasses off, looked around some more, and then put them back on. Shelby couldn't help but think this was a woman with a schedule to keep, and it made her wonder what was up. Fantasies began to pop into Shelby's head, fantasies about spies and intrigue, and she had to wonder if this woman had something to do with Shelby's vacation. The woman's tight black T-shirt did nothing to stem the tide of Shelby's overactive imagination.

Once she was finally clear of the other passengers trying to leave the confines of the train, Shelby caught sight of the woman again, still looking around the platform as though she was nervous about something. It didn't take her long to figure out who the mystery babe was looking for. As Shelby jumped down from the last step of the train to the concrete of the platform, the woman approached her.

"You are Shelby Hutchinson, no?" the woman asked in a heavily accented voice.

"Um, no...er, yeah, I mean. I'm Shelby Hutchinson. Who are you?"

"Later." The woman began pulling her toward the exit. "Right now you need to come with me."

Shelby wasn't about to go running off with a stranger, especially when that stranger's accent sounded decidedly Russian and Shelby's trip was supposed to include shooting at Russian spies. She planted both feet, resolutely crossed her arms over her chest, and tried again to find out this woman's true identity.

"Now, wait just a second here. I don't even know who you are."

"I will explain, but later. Right now, we must leave."

As much as she wanted to argue, Shelby spotted something that quickly changed her mind. Two men appeared from around the corner of the rail terminal. Goon Number One was decked in a trench coat and fedora, Goon Number Two in a black suit. Both looked every bit the clichéd picture of the KGB agents from her video games. "Oh, shit..." was all she managed to say as she watched Goon Number Two reach under his black jacket and pull out a pistol. That was all she needed to see.

The woman broke into a run. Shelby followed, pretty sure the goons were after her, even though she wasn't completely sure why. She allowed a small smile as she ran after the woman in the leather jacket. This was exactly what she had paid for, and she wasn't about to blow it by standing on the platform and asking too many questions. By the time Shelby got to the steps that led down to the street, her mystery woman was already pulling on a helmet and getting ready to start a motorcycle. Shelby caught up, and the woman tossed her a second helmet, which Shelby put on while the woman climbed on the bike and cranked it up.

Shelby quickly climbed on the back of the motorcycle, tightened the shoulder strap on her duffel bag, and held on tight.

Shelby closed her eyes and let out a long breath as the motorcycle pulled away from the curb and into the busy traffic of West Berlin. Undaunted by the fact she had no idea where they were headed, Shelby just hung on, glad to be transported away from the goons with the guns. Her relief was short-lived as she spotted the men getting into a black BMW parked illegally near the entrance to the West Berlin Station. The mystery woman must have seen them too. She gave the bike some gas, wove her way dangerously through the traffic, and sped past a sign Shelby recognized from her research as an entrance for the autobahn. Once on the major freeway, the woman seriously cranked up the gas, forcing Shelby to hang on even tighter. She had no idea how fast they were going, but she was certain it was faster than what normally would be considered safe for two women and a rather heavy duffel bag on a motorcycle.

The woman dodged in and out of traffic, changing lanes as needed to maintain her speed. It didn't take Shelby long to get the hang of leaning with the motion of the bike and she eventually got comfortable enough to risk removing one hand from the woman's midsection to tighten the strap of her duffel bag enough to keep it from swinging loose with each lean of the motorcycle. She looked around as the sights of West Berlin sped by and wondered if she might get a chance to roam around the city. Well, that wasn't actually the point of her trip, so Shelby stopped musing about all touristy kinds of stuff, returned her free arm to the woman's waist, and held on.

Shelby braved a look to try to see the speedometer on the motorcycle but gave it up when she noticed motion in the rearview mirror on the right side of the bike. It was the black BMW from the train station and it was closing fast. The mystery woman must have seen it too, as she increased her speed to maintain the distance between them and the goons in the car. Shelby closed her eyes and tucked her head in behind the woman's back. She didn't even know how tightly she had been hanging on until she realized, over the noise of the engine and the wind, that the woman was trying to talk to her.

"Shoot the tires," she said over her shoulder.

"What…me…huh…?" Shelby stammered.

"*Da*, you. Shoot their tires."

"But I don't have a gun."

"No gun." The woman seemed unfazed. She grabbed Shelby's right hand and pulled it closer under her left breast toward the weapon Shelby found holstered there. "Use mine."

Despite the fact Shelby had never fired a real gun in her life, she pulled the weapon from its holster and tried to turn around. From her seat on the back of the bike, going close to a hundred miles an hour, once again hanging on with only one hand, she couldn't even hold the gun still, much less fire it with any approximation of accuracy. Blowing a hole in the windshield of a car loaded with Mom, Dad, kids, and the family dog sounded like a terrible idea, so rather than shoot wildly and hope for the best, Shelby begged off.

"I can't. I don't know what to do."

The woman reached back, took the gun from Shelby's hand, and said, "You drive."

"What? Me?" Shelby squeaked, more than a little panicked, but it was too late. The woman returned the gun to its holster, grabbed Shelby's right hand, and placed it on the accelerator. The bike wiggled precariously while Shelby reached around and got her left hand situated on the other handlebar grip. "Oh, shit." She tried to figure out how to balance two people on a motorcycle. Just as she had decided it wasn't that hard, she heard a crack somewhere from behind, followed quickly by a second and then a third. She braved a quick glance in the rearview mirror again and noticed the passenger in the black BMW was now leaning out of his window, shooting a gun in their general direction.

"Oh, double shit." Shelby clenched her jaw and tried not to freak when the woman reached under her jacket and pulled her gun out for the second time. She then twisted to get under Shelby's left arm and leaned over, facing the car behind them, leaving Shelby to drive from the back of the motorcycle while she shot at the front tires of the BMW. The gun discharged twice with loud pops, followed almost instantaneously by a different kind of pop as the left front tire of the BMW exploded, throwing the car out of control and into the guardrail. Shelby blew out a long breath as the woman reached into her jacket to return the weapon to its holster, and then sat up to take over control of the motorcycle.

"Oh, God help me…" was all Shelby had left to say, as she closed her eyes, squeezed even tighter, and willed herself not to pee her pants. She let out another long breath as the woman changed lanes and slowed to a speed Shelby felt a little more comfortable with. They traveled in silence for another fifteen minutes, speeding past the outer edge of West Berlin, until the woman finally eased off the gas and downshifted, slowing enough to take the ramp that would lead them off the autobahn. She doubled back and began to weave her way through a series of side streets and alleys, taking Shelby God knew where. She could only assume the woman knew where they were going, so she just held on and hoped they would stop soon. That little trip down the autobahn had been more than enough excitement to hold her for a while.

The woman finally stopped the motorcycle in front of an old building off a dingy back street somewhere in the outskirts of West Berlin. As she climbed off the bike and removed her helmet, Shelby watched a healthy-looking rat scurry away from an overflowing trash bin to disappear into a crack at the foundation of a nearby building. She shuddered and thought again she probably should have allowed Andrew to explain all of the details of her trip, but let it go once she realized that ship had long since sailed.

With no idea where they were, Shelby didn't have much choice but to trust the woman who was leading her into the building and up three flights of stairs. The woman dug through the pockets of her jeans and then pulled out a key to unlock the first door at the top of the steps. She gestured for Shelby to enter the small apartment first and checked over her shoulder one last time before she followed Shelby through the door, closing and locking it behind her.

Shelby just stood there while the woman checked the windows and closets. She was finally calming down from the harrowing ride on the motorcycle as the woman turned toward her. "This place is safe for you."

"What?" Shelby still had no clue about anything that was happening, so she tried again to find out what the heck was going on. "Who are you?"

"I am Tasha. I am to help you," she answered in the thick Russian accent Shelby was beginning to believe was the sexiest thing she had ever heard. But Shelby was still puzzled.

"Okay. Help me what?"

Tasha crossed her arms over her ample breasts and stared in a way Shelby believed meant she might have thought Shelby was nuts.

"You are Shelby Hutchinson, correct?"

"Yes, I am Shelby Hutchinson."

"And you work for United States CIA. You are a courier, no?"

"No...I mean, yes. Wait, I'm not...well, maybe. Sorry, I'm not sure." Shelby shrugged, attempting to piece together a response that made any sense at all.

"You do not know if you are courier?"

"Well, I suppose I am." Shelby swallowed her fear. "What does it mean if I am?"

Tasha continued to stare at Shelby, looking her up and down in a way that made Shelby more than a little nervous. "If you are a courier, it means you are a lousy courier that can't shoot a gun and it means also what you have in the bag is for me to help you with."

"What, this bag?" Shelby asked as she pulled the shoulder strap for the duffel over her head and set the bag on the floor. "It's just my luggage."

"Just your luggage." Tasha laughed a little, but Shelby had no idea why. "Are you certain of that?"

"Well, no. I just assumed…"

"Ah, be careful what you assume, Shelby Hutchinson." Tasha reached down to unzip Shelby's duffel bag, then pulled out T-shirts, socks, and underpants and tossed them aside.

Shelby gasped and stepped back, trying to get as far away from the contents of her luggage as she could manage. She had no idea what she was looking at, but she was sure it wasn't tampons and shampoo. It looked more like two to three feet of black PVC pipe broken down into small, manageable sections with some mysterious buttons, dials, a scope, and a trigger.

"What the fuck is that?" she asked.

"That, Shelby Hutchinson, is a prototype grenade launcher, and I am to help you deliver it to operatives in the Soviet Union."

"Oh, shit." Shelby ran the fingers of both hands nervously through her hair.

"Oh, shit is right, and I think you need my help very much." Tasha hesitated, looking deeply into Shelby's eyes. "Especially if you want to stay alive."

"Alive?" Shelby stared wide-eyed as Tasha knelt to examine the duffel bag on the floor. She was fine, really, until Tasha poked one finger through a hole in the black canvas, showing Shelby two very neat little bullet holes, one in and one out of the fabric. Shelby offered one last "oh, shit" as everything got fuzzy. Darkness closed in as her eyes rolled up into her head and she collapsed to the floor in a dead faint.

Chapter Three

Shelby awoke, unsure of her surroundings and more than a little confused. The last thing she remembered was it was just beginning to get dark outside, and then there was the thing with the... Oh shit, there was a grenade launcher in the duffel bag. Oh, yeah. And two bullet holes as well. Ooh, that was bad, but it was all coming back to her slowly. She knew it was late April, so the light streaming in the windows of the apartment looked to her like the bright rays of midmorning, but since she didn't have a clock next to the bed, she had no idea of the exact time. "Wait a minute. I'm in bed and I'm..." Shelby sat up and yanked on the sheets to look under the covers. Since she had absolutely no idea of how she wound up in bed, she prayed she hadn't been up and talking to anyone wearing nothing but a white tank top, pink socks, and red and white candy-striped panties. That would have been bad.

She heard a key in the lock of the door and yelped, pulling the covers up around her neck. Tasha was back, and she was bearing breakfast. Shelby hoped it was breakfast anyway, as her stomach rumbled unhappily.

"Ah, Shelby Hutchinson, you are finally awake. I thought you would sleep until Great October Socialist Revolution Day. You had big day yesterday, no?" Tasha began pulling baked goods from a white paper sack. "I assume you are hungry."

Shelby patted her tummy. "Yeah, I didn't get dinner, so I'm starving. What's for breakfast?"

"Since you are a big tough American courier, I brought for you coffee and brötchen." Shelby had to laugh at Tasha's attempt at sarcasm as Tasha handed her a Styrofoam cup. "You must eat."

Shelby wasn't about to argue with that as she peeled off the plastic top from her coffee and took a long sniff of the sludgy dark brew. "Mmm…coffee." She wrapped her hands around the cup and blew across the top. "What exactly is brötchen?"

"Brötchen is what you eat for breakfast in Berlin. It's bread that's like a hand grenade, how you say, chewy."

"Sounds yummy. Why don't you pass me one of those yeast-raised hand grenades there, Tasha?" Shelby scrunched up her nose as she set her coffee on the nightstand and accepted a chunk of bread. "I hope it was you that undressed me and put me to bed."

Tasha smiled again as she defended her honor with an open palm held to her own chest. "*Da*, but I was a perfect gentleman. You fainted, so I took your clothes off you and put you in bed." Tasha pointed across the room, drawing Shelby's gaze to her jeans and sweatshirt, neatly folded in a stack on top of the dresser. "You are feeling better now, yes?"

"Yes, thank you, I am. Oh, and my fractured honor thanks you too."

Shelby reached for her coffee on the nightstand. She sipped tentatively at the steaming brew in an attempt to try to wash down a particularly chewy piece of brötchen, and allowed a small pang of regret. It was a shame she had been stripped darn near naked, carried to bed, and tucked in by a gorgeous Russian babe wearing a leather jacket and shoulder holster, and she was completely unaware of the whole thing. When Shelby finally looked up, she noticed the smile had faded from Tasha's face.

"As for honor, Shelby Hutchinson, it's time for truth. You are most definitely not a courier for the CIA. Certainly not like one ever seen by me." Tasha was serious now. Shelby could hear the change in the tone of her voice.

"Well, yeah, about that…" Shelby hesitated long enough to drink a little more coffee before she continued. "It's a long story, and I'm not sure you'd believe me if I told you. But you said you were here to help me. Will you still help me?"

Tasha nodded, a move that served to alleviate much of Shelby's anxiety about the task at hand. "*Da*, I will help you, but first I must know some things."

Shelby arched her eyebrows over her coffee cup, silently encouraging Tasha to begin the quiz.

"Do you know how to shoot a gun?"

Shelby quickly shook her head and stared into her coffee.

"Okay, then, can you fight?"

Shelby looked up and shrugged. She could easily see from Tasha's furrowed brow that she was getting frustrated.

"Can you drive a car?"

"Yes," Shelby blurted out, happy to finally be able to answer something positively. "I learned to drive a car when I was sixteen. Of course, I've lived in downtown Chicago for six years, and I only take the train or walk, and I never leave the city, so it has been a while. I don't even own a car."

"Oh, Shelby Hutchinson, I don't think I believe you. The Politburo tells Soviet comrades all Americans have two cars in their driveway."

"Well, I don't have a car or a driveway, so I think your Politburo is full of beans."

Tasha looked confused. "Beans? What do beans have to do with cars?"

"No, no…not real beans. It's just an expression that means I think your Politburo is incorrect."

"Oh, like when a person is full with shit," Tasha said.

"Full of shit."

"Ah, full of shit," Tasha repeated. "I understand. Thank you."

"You're welcome." Shelby smiled nervously. "So will you please help me?"

"*Da*, I will help you." Tasha set her tea on the nightstand next to Shelby's coffee and put her palms on her thighs as she stood and turned to face the bed. "But that means there is much to show you today since we must leave tomorrow for the Soviet Union. Eat your brötchen, put on your clothes, then we go and I'll teach you to shoot a gun and fight."

Shelby smiled as she tossed the covers aside and got up to get dressed. This was going to be fun.

Twenty minutes later, despite Shelby's eager preparations to get out the door, she was getting more and more frustrated. While she had managed to get her shoes tied and the Velcro straps tightened around her ankles, she was still wrestling with the buttons on her way-too-tight jeans. "How the fuck?"

"You must lie down on the bed and hold your breath. That is the only way." Tasha lightly pushed Shelby back toward the mattress. "You cannot learn to fight in tight American Levi jeans. We must get you something else."

"Ooh, I have money and a credit card. We can go shopping." She lay back on the bed, held her breath, and managed to get the buttons done up on her jeans.

"It's a good idea, Shelby Hutchinson. We must leave soon, yes?"

"Yes, I'm ready, but what about…you know…" Shelby didn't even want to mention what was sitting in her duffel bag, so she opted to stop talking and point, hoping Tasha would understand.

"Ah, the prototype grenade launcher. It's okay here. We can lock the door and I have the only key." Tasha slid the duffel under the bed with her boot-clad foot. "It's safe."

"Well, that's just dandy. Then I think we should be going."

Shelby felt great as she pounded down three flights of stairs and pushed her way out the door and into the street. It was a sunny, glorious morning, and everything was working out even better than she had hoped. She had wanted to find excitement, a break from her mundane every day, and now she was right in the middle of it with a hot babe in tow to boot. The sound of the door closing behind her made Shelby turn around and watch Tasha as she pulled on her helmet. Shelby was happy to have an ally who seemed to know exactly what do. That was a nice thing to have.

A short time later, Shelby found herself leaving a sporting goods store loaded down with sweatpants, an open-necked sweatshirt, legwarmers, and an aqua headband, of all things. She liked the scrunchy socks that matched the headband, though. They were going to look cute peeking out of her high-tops. At least that's what the salesgirl had said. Shelby also made a quick mental note to look up what the heck the word "flashdance" meant when she returned home. She followed Tasha back toward the motorcycle, enjoying the sunshine of a warm April day and thanking Jake for talking her into this whole Head Trip vacation thing when her attention was captured by something in a shop window. "Hey, Tasha. What do you think? Can I pull off the leather jacket thing?"

"Ah, Shelby Hutchinson, I think you are capable of anything you want." Tasha offered Shelby a gentle smile. "You should go inside to look, maybe even put it on to see."

Shelby wasn't sold yet. "I'm not sure. It's kind of...oh, I don't know."

"If you do not have a jacket, you should get one. It's still cold at night." Shelby wrinkled her brow. "Go in, Shelby Hutchinson. Put on the jacket. It'll make you look like an American tough guy."

This gal was good. Shelby bit her lip, finally convinced to go in and look at the black leather bomber.

Ten minutes later, after a substantial hit to her Visa card, Shelby stepped back out into the noontime sunshine. She stopped to show off her purchase, more than a little puffed up about her new look. Tasha smiled, so Shelby smiled too as Tasha pulled at the front of the new jacket, straightening it.

"See, you do look tough. Like a badass courier in a spy movie. I like it," Tasha said with a waggle of her eyebrows.

"Really?" Shelby squeaked in response. She could have sworn Tasha was flirting with her. Well, even if she wasn't, Shelby was feeling decidedly good about herself right about now.

"*Da*, really, Shelby Hutchinson. I'll teach you to fight and then I'll be afraid of you too." Tasha pulled her closer to whisper, "Also, last night, when you were asleep, I talked to an old comrade and got you a gun. The jacket will be good for cover."

"No kidding? Where is it? Let me see…" Shelby was practically bouncing on the sidewalk in her white aerobic high-tops.

"Ah, not yet. This is not a good place. You must have patience."

Shelby tried to conceal her disappointment. Patience had never been one of her virtues, but she also didn't want to push too hard. "Okay, I'll be patient. Can we go now? I think I'm finally ready to try and kick some butt."

Tasha pulled Shelby along, back toward the motorcycle. Once Shelby's purchases were secure, Tasha cranked up the bike while Shelby climbed on the back. She held on as Tasha gunned the engine and released the clutch, pulling into the light flow of midday traffic.

Shelby hoped it wouldn't take long to get wherever they were going. She still had no idea exactly where she was, and now she knew Tasha had found her a gun, and she hoped a nifty shoulder holster too. Then she would look like Tasha's "badass courier." While she had a promise of assistance from her, Shelby was beginning to wonder where this was all leading. She knew the grenade launcher had to go to somewhere in the Soviet Union, but still had no idea who she was giving it to, or worse, what they would do with it once they had it. And there were still the goons from the train station. Would there be more? She had to assume so, especially considering Tasha's warning about needing some skills to stay alive. Maybe after she learned to fight and shoot she could risk asking Tasha some questions.

As Tasha drove, Shelby held on tightly. This trip was less action packed than yesterday's high velocity flight down the autobahn, but Shelby held on tight anyway. She was quickly coming to realize the woman who was now helping her was also filling her head with a series of images that were playing havoc with Shelby's own overactive imagination. Tasha's toned, flat belly felt nice under her hands, even through the T-shirt she was wearing, and Shelby found that she wondered how the rest of Tasha's body might feel. She imagined wrestling around on the floor as Tasha taught her how to defend herself. The fantasy continued as Shelby thought about what it would feel like to be pinned to the floor by this amazingly attractive woman. How it would feel as she straddled Shelby's prone form, and how Tasha just wouldn't be able to help herself as she held Shelby's hands over her head and leaned down to kiss her. All fun things to think about, but Shelby decided to stow it away for now as Tasha brought the bike to a stop in front of another building down yet another back street.

Shelby looked up and down the front of the building. She couldn't read the German printing on the sign, but she did recognize the odd characters below the German words as Korean text. "What is this place?"

Tasha opened the compartment under the seat of the bike and pulled out a small black nylon bag. "Ah, it's a school for self-defense and belongs to an old comrade. He said we may use it for today."

Shelby thought about the gun and the martial arts school. "Wow, you have some interesting comrades, don't you?"

"*Da*, Shelby Hutchinson, I know many people here. Come, we have much to do."

Shelby followed like a puppy, eager to find out what Tasha had in store for her. Once inside, Tasha found the light switch and pointed Shelby toward the changing rooms. Shelby dug through her bags, found a pair of sweatpants for Tasha, tossed them toward her, and headed off to change. It struck Shelby as a little odd when Tasha didn't follow her into the changing room, but she understood why as soon as she returned to the large room with the mats on the floor. She could see through the large glass window separating the office from the training room that Tasha was on the telephone and she didn't seem happy. The details of the conversation were unavailable to Shelby since she didn't speak Russian, but Tasha was definitely agitated. After one last particularly angry-sounding flurry of Russian, Shelby flinched as Tasha slammed the phone down, took a long breath, and turned to leave the office.

Since Shelby didn't want to appear as if she had been eavesdropping, she flopped down on the floor and began stretching her legs. As Tasha approached, shrugging out of her jacket on the way, Shelby looked up and asked, "Is everything okay?"

"*Da*, Shelby Hutchinson, all is okay." Shelby continued to stretch as she watched Tasha cross her toned arms over her chest and clench her jaw. "Comrade Boris is being, how do you say, a large asshole." Shelby spit out a laugh and quickly slapped one hand over her own mouth. "What is so funny?"

Shelby couldn't seem to stop the giggles despite her best attempts. "Sorry. You just said something about Boris, and all I could think about was Boris and Natasha, these two characters from an old cartoon I used to watch on DVDs at my grandma's house, and it made me want to say something about moose and squirrel." Shelby was laughing even harder now.

"Moose and squirrel?" Once Shelby heard the words in Tasha's Russian accent, there was no hope her hysterics would subside anytime soon. Shelby wrapped her arms around her midsection and fell over backward on the mat, howling with laughter.

"Please, Tasha, say it again."

HEAD TRIP

"What? Moose and squirrel?"

Shelby was a goner. She had nothing left but to pull her knees up and roll on the floor, crippled by paroxysms of laughter. While tears flowed freely down her face, Shelby struggled to breathe and try to regain some semblance of control. She was fine until she looked up at Tasha, an action that served to start the whole cycle over again.

Tasha wasn't laughing. She just stood there, arms crossed. "Shelby Hutchinson, you are a crazy person. What is so funny and what is DVD?"

As she finally began to calm down, Shelby wiped at her eyes and tried to piece together an answer to both questions. "Okay, there was this cartoon about a moose named Bullwinkle and his buddy was a squirrel named Rocky. There were these two Russian spies named Boris and Natasha who were always chasing after moose and squirrel. I just thought it was funny. And DVD is just something my grandma used to call the videos she had." Shelby lied, but just a little since she realized DVDs hadn't been invented yet.

Tasha seemed mollified, at least for the moment. "Okay, but I still think you are a crazy person."

"Well, maybe. It's certainly not the first time I've been accused of that."

"Why does this not surprise me?"

Shelby shrugged. "Considering everything else that's happened since you found me yesterday, I think it only makes sense you would think I was crazy. I mean, I'm supposed to be this big, badass CIA courier, and it turns out I can't shoot a gun, and let's not forget about the fainting at the sight of bullet holes thing. I'd be surprised if you thought anything else."

"*Da*, that makes much sense to me." Tasha continued to stare, until she seemed to come to a decision to let it all go. "So, Shelby Hutchinson, are you ready to show me what you are able to do?"

"Um, sure." Shelby wasn't certain she was ready to display the true depth of her ineptitude to Tasha, but hey, no time like the present. "What should I do?"

"Hit me," Tasha said as she motioned toward her own face with her hands.

"What?" Shelby couldn't believe her ears.

"You heard me, Shelby Hutchinson. I want you to try to hit me."

"But I don't want to hurt you."

"I am fine. Please, you try."

"Well, okay…" Shelby balled up her fists and struck the closest approximation of a boxing pose she could manage. Still, she wasn't certain about throwing a punch for real, so she dropped her hands to her sides. "Are you sure?"

"*Da*, is time to stop with fooling around."

"Okay, if that's what you want." Shelby danced around a little while she pulled her fists up for the second time, took a deep breath, closed her eyes, and swung as hard as she could. Not surprisingly, she met with nothing but air as Tasha neatly dodged the blow. With no way to stop her forward momentum, Shelby spun around like a top and tripped over her own feet, landing on her butt on the mat-covered floor with a dull "oof."

As Shelby tried to scrape together what was left of her pride, she looked up to see that Tasha was biting her own lip, in what Shelby could only assume was an attempt not to laugh. Tasha held a hand out to help her up. "That was, how do you say, smooth."

Shelby accepted the assistance. "Well, yeah. Sorry, that was pretty lame. I suppose you aren't terribly surprised to find out I'm a huge spaz in addition to being a lousy courier."

"It's okay, Shelby Hutchinson. It's only your first try. You will do better next time. Try again, but keep your eyes open this time."

"Okay." Shelby got back into her boxing stance and prepared to swing again. The results were much the same as she swung and missed, only this time she managed to avoid landing hard on the floor when Tasha caught her around the middle and held her up. Despite the fact she was starting to feel like a complete idiot, Shelby couldn't help but notice how strong Tasha was. The well-muscled arms around her waist, holding her from behind felt awfully good. Maybe a little too good, since Shelby found she wasn't in any hurry to extricate herself from the embrace.

It didn't appear as if Tasha was in any hurry to let her go either. "Shelby Hutchinson, I think you are not paying attention to the fight."

Shelby held the arms against her, trying to make it look like she needed more help. It was obvious she needed more help, but thoughts of learning to fight were quickly slipping away with the last shards of Shelby's shattered dignity. She nodded while she struggled to come up with something witty to say. Hell, anything to say was better than just standing there, but the warm body wrapped around her back was playing havoc with her senses. She closed her eyes against the barrage of feelings. "Yeah, I'm having a little trouble here, um…concentrating."

"*Da*, I noticed that."

Shelby could swear she detected a bit of reluctance once Tasha finally did let her go, turning her around to take her by the upper arms. "Shelby Hutchinson, this is important. There are people, many people, who wish to keep you from your task and will stop at nothing to do so. I am afraid for you."

Shelby found that as much as she wanted this attention, it was proving to be more than a little overwhelming. She let her gaze drift to the floor. "I know, Tasha. I get that. It's just…"

"It's just what?"

"It's just…well…never mind." Shelby pulled herself together as she waved off Tasha's concerned look. She squared her shoulders, straightened out her tank top, and dug deep to find some resolve to continue. "Let's try this again, but maybe you could show me something else besides the spin-around-and-fall-on-my-ass-like-a-dork maneuver."

From the set of Tasha's jaw and the look in her eye, Shelby

could see that she was thinking, trying to come up with a new idea. "Do you know about a Japanese fighting technique called aikido?" Shelby shook her head. "It's a kind of fighting that uses the attacker's own, what is the word…movement against them."

"How about if you just show me?"

"Okay, this I can do. You come at me slowly." Tasha encouraged Shelby to move, gesturing toward herself with both hands. Shelby did as instructed, coming in low and slow. Rather than try to stop her, Tasha pushed, directing Shelby's momentum to the side, forcing her to pass by harmlessly. The huge math and physics geek inside Shelby got the point immediately.

"Oh, I get it. It's the redirection of inertia." Tasha screwed up her face as though she didn't understand. "It's like this. Inertia is the principle wherein an object in motion tends to remain in motion until acted upon by an outside force. You're teaching me to be the outside force. That is so cool!"

"*Da*, that is exactly what I am showing you. Try again, only faster."

"All right." Shelby had a newfound sense of confidence. She lowered her head, charged, and immediately found herself airborne, feet up and head down, right before she landed flat on her back. From her spot on the floor, Shelby tried to catch the breath that had just been knocked from her. "Wow, I didn't see that one coming." Tasha reached down to give Shelby a helping hand up.

"Are you okay, Shelby Hutchinson?"

"Yeah, I think so." Shelby accepted the assistance, pulled herself to her feet, dusted off her sweatpants, and glared at Tasha. "How about a little warning next time, okay?"

"I am sorry, but you must learn, and sometimes it's necessary to do the, how do you say, hard way. You try now, okay?"

Shelby was mollified, at least for the moment. "Okay. I'm ready."

Tasha lowered her head and charged with a roar. Shelby yelped in response and at the appropriate moment, shoved with all her might, knocking Tasha off course and off her feet at the same time. As she tumbled all the way over and popped up on her feet, Tasha smiled and nodded her head. "*Da*, Shelby Hutchinson. That is the right idea."

"That was so cool! Can we try again?"

"*Da*, we will do that again, many times." With no additional warning, she charged again, and Shelby responded. And again, like promised, many more times. Just for good measure, Tasha switched it up and had Shelby charge, demonstrating how force plus leverage equals one bad guy flying through the air to land on his ass. Shelby was elated. Every time she managed to get Tasha airborne, Shelby would squeal with delight, until one mistimed application of leverage sent Tasha out of control to land hard on the mat.

"Oh, shit, Tasha. Are you okay? I'm sorry, I didn't mean, I mean I thought, well, I didn't think, I just did, and you were all wonky with the half-gainer and all. I'm so sorry…"

"It's not a big deal. It's like, how do you say, shit is happening."

"Shit happens," Shelby said as she went over to offer a hand up from the mat. Tasha accepted the hand, but instead of pulling herself up, she pulled Shelby down to her. Before she even knew what hit her, Shelby was on her back on the floor, pinned to the mat by Tasha, who was now straddling Shelby's midsection with knees on either side of her waist. "What the…?"

"Ah, Shelby Hutchinson. When you knock a bad guy on his butt, run away." Shelby nodded, wide-eyed, as Tasha leaned forward to pin her hands to the mat on either side of her head. "You must always run away, okay?"

"What if I don't want to run away?" Shelby decided she wasn't going anywhere anytime soon. Tasha leaned forward and Shelby could feel her smooth tummy through the fabric of her shirt, the delicious pressure as Tasha's breasts flattened against her own.

Shelby felt breath, mere inches from her mouth, and heard

Tasha say, "Are you sure you should not be running away now, Shelby Hutchinson?"

Shelby shook her head. "I'm not going anywhere."

"Good." Shelby felt the distance close between her mouth and those lovely Russian lips. She licked her own lips in preparation, but got nothing but a loud noise as the front door of the studio burst open and a deep male voice called out.

"Natasha?"

"Oh shit."

Tasha mouthed a single word in Russian that Shelby guessed meant something similar to what she had just said. "Who is that?" she asked.

"Shh." Tasha released one of Shelby's hands to cover her mouth. "It's Boris. Shit."

Since she wasn't able to speak, Shelby stared back, scared half to death, wondering what the hell was going on.

But Tasha had a plan. "Stay low. Go to the changing room. Lock the door and wait for me. I will knock three times when the coast is clear, okay?"

Shelby nodded, too panicked to offer much else, and rolled onto her knees to crawl back toward the changing room. Once there, she closed the door, cringing against the click of the latch as she slid the bolt to lock the door. From the safety of the changing room, Shelby blew out a long breath and dropped to the floor with her back against the wall. She hugged her knees close, struggled to control her breathing to keep from hyperventilating, and waited for Tasha to knock.

Chapter Four

S helby wasn't sure how long she sat curled up on the floor in the changing room. It could have been hours as far as she knew, but she didn't have a watch, so it remained a mystery. After what seemed like an unusually long time, Shelby startled to the sound of three soft raps on the door. She jumped up, unlocked the door, and pulled it open, hiding behind it as Tasha pushed her way into the room.

"Are you okay, Shelby Hutchinson?" Shelby nodded as Tasha closed the door behind her. "Good. We have only a few minutes. I told Comrade Boris I needed to use the bathroom, so he is still here. We have to get you out of here."

"What? Leave? Why? Tasha, what the hell is going on?" The last thing Shelby wanted at this point was to be separated from Tasha. Especially considering Tasha had been about one breath away from kissing her when Boris showed up. Talk about lousy timing.

Tasha didn't budge. "I will tell you everything, but it must be later. Right now, you need to head back to the apartment. Go out the window, down the alley, and out to big street. There you will be able to find a taxicab. Tell the driver to take you to Einundsechzig, that is sixty-one in English, Libauer Strasse. I will meet you there soon. Can you remember this?"

Shelby nodded her understanding. Leaving was not her first

choice, but she also knew, deep down, she didn't have much of an option. Tasha stopped her as Shelby picked up her new jacket. "Wait, I have a gun and holster for you." She pulled out a medium-sized handgun, wrapped in a holster and shoulder straps, from her black nylon bag. Tasha helped Shelby into the rig, showed her where the extra magazines were located, and began to give her the seriously condensed version of Soviet pistol training.

"This is a Makarov PM." Tasha held the weapon out for Shelby to see.

Shelby immediately recognized the semiautomatic handgun from her video game back home. "Yeah, I know. It's the standard-issue sidearm for the Soviet Red Army." A look of disbelief crossed Tasha's face. "What? I'm not a total idiot. I do know some things, you know."

"Of course. I am sorry." Shelby could hear the sincerity in Tasha's voice, but it was gone quickly, replaced by a military-style detachment. "Anyway, this button releases the magazine." Tasha demonstrated, pulling the magazine free of the gun. "So you can see it's also loaded. Slide it in, like this." She locked the magazine in place with the palm of her hand. "It has double action, so you can keep it in the holster, and it's always ready to shoot. Point the gun away from you. Pull the trigger. The gun goes bang and the bad guy goes down." She handed over the Makarov. "Do you understand, Shelby Hutchinson?"

"Yes, I understand." Shelby slid the weapon back into its new home under her left arm and snapped the strap closed to keep it secure. "Taxi to Einundsechzig Libauer Strasse. You'll meet me there soon. Makarov PM. Don't shoot myself in the foot. Got it."

Tasha helped Shelby shrug into her leather jacket. "Also, keep your jacket zipped to cover the Makarov." She dug in her pockets and pulled out a key, which she handed to Shelby. "Here is the key for the apartment. I will knock three times again. Now go, Shelby Hutchinson, and please be careful, yes?"

"Hey, it's me," Shelby said with a weak grin.

"That is why I am worried."

"Smart ass." Shelby turned to grab her bags and climb out the window. "You be careful too, please."

"I am always careful, Shelby Hutchinson."

Shelby felt hands on her butt pushing her headfirst out the window and into the adjacent alley. Once back on her feet, she turned right, as instructed, and trotted out toward the bigger street and the safety of a taxi. One whistle and a friendly wave later and Shelby had a ride. The driver asked her destination and she quoted back, "Einundsechzig Libauer Strasse, please...I mean *bitte*."

The driver confirmed the order with a nod and pulled slowly into traffic. Shelby finally had a couple of seconds to think, which was good because she had lots of things to think about. Russians named Boris and Natasha, one very mysterious and one with a truly fine ass, although no less mysterious. She could only shake her head and wonder what was going on with Tasha. Enigmatic promises of "later" to Shelby's questions were proving to be more than a little disconcerting, but Shelby couldn't deny her attraction to the cryptic, yet drop-dead gorgeous Tasha.

Shelby had to laugh to herself. Maybe "drop-dead" wasn't a great choice of words, considering the guns and the motorcycles and the grenade launcher. She also had to consider who was attracted to whom. The near kiss, after all, hadn't been Shelby's idea, now, had it? And what about Tasha's invisible comrades? Heavily armed martial arts studio owners, and who knew what else besides the mystery comrade named Boris who had shown up looking for Tasha. Shelby was puzzled, especially considering the fact only an hour or so earlier, Tasha had growled at Boris and hung up the phone on him.

Yep, Shelby was puzzled all right. But she was also hungry. A shining pair of Golden Arches drew Shelby's attention. Wow, she hadn't been in or even seen a McDonald's since she was a little kid in 2021 when the World Health Organization shut down every last one of the fast food chain's establishments shortly after declaring them to be a public health hazard.

Shelby didn't care. She wanted a Big Mac.

The cab driver parked by the curb and waited while Shelby ran inside. Five minutes later, she was back in the cab clutching a bright white bag of nutritionally bereft joy and a Coke in a cup the size of a small wastebasket. Ten minutes after that, Shelby was standing in the middle of Libauer Strasse, watching the cab's taillights as they disappeared around the corner. She wanted to laugh as she looked down at the image she presented—shopping and food bags in one hand, monster drink in the other, and someone else's Makarov, loaded and stowed under her brand-new leather jacket. Lots of changes in a couple of days, and Shelby was a little overwhelmed. Food and a bit of rest would fix that, so she made her way up to the apartment. There was a television in the living room and she turned it on for some mindless company, then sat cross-legged on the bed to eat.

That's where she was, two and a half hours later, struggling to watch classic *Star Trek* dubbed in German, when she heard three light taps on the door. Shelby bounded from the bed to unlock and open the door and Tasha pushed her way into the small apartment.

"Oh good, Shelby Hutchinson, you are safe. I was concerned."

"Why? Is something wrong?"

"*Nyet*, all is okay." Tasha set her black nylon bag on the dresser, looked around the room, and shrugged out of her jacket. "Is the grenade launcher also okay?"

Shelby hadn't even thought to check on the condition of the grenade launcher, so she pulled out her duffel bag and discovered quickly all was well there too. She breathed out a sigh of relief and noted a noise behind her that sounded as though Tasha had reacted the same way.

Shelby stood to face her. "Tasha, what's going on?"

"What? Everything is okay." Tasha looked away to toss her jacket onto a nearby chair.

There it was again. No real answer to her question, so Shelby pushed a little harder. "No, that's not what I meant. I know we're supposed to take the grenade launcher somewhere else, but you're being all cagey Russian agent, or whatever the heck you are, and then there's the angry phone call, Boris shows up, and you're all with the shoving my skinny butt out the window. What gives, Tasha?"

"Gives? I am not giving anything."

"No, no. Sorry. It's just another expression that means I don't understand what we're doing here. Every time I ask you what's going on, you promise to tell me later. Well, it's later, and I want to know what we're doing here."

Shelby could see Tasha was getting frustrated as well. "Shelby Hutchinson, you were also not being truthful with me. You say you are a courier, and you are here with the prototype grenade launcher, but you have no weapons, no help, no plan." Tasha ticked off the points with her fingers. "What is it you want me to believe?"

Shelby had no idea how to answer that question. Any nonsense she could cook up about being an adventure seeker from the future wasn't going to fly. Add to that the fact she was out of her element and trying to pretend to be something she wasn't left her with a huge problem. Shelby was screwed and had no choice but to try to convince Tasha to blindly trust her.

"Okay, here's the best way I have to explain it. I'm here as a challenge. I know some people who know some other people, and so here I am."

Tasha clearly wasn't buying it, offering a small snort as her response. "I do not believe you."

"Well, it's the best I have, so maybe you'll just have to trust me."

"So, Shelby Hutchinson, I am to trust you with nothing but a lame story, but you will not do the same for me?"

"Okay, Tasha, you're right about that, so I need to trust you. And I do, but help me a little, okay? You're very obviously Russian, you have Russian friends, and you carry Red Army–issue weapons. It's equally obvious I'm an American, and I thought that meant we were supposed to be on different sides. Why are you helping me?"

"Ah, Shelby Hutchinson, it is just like when you were telling me that the Politburo was full with beans about all Americans having two cars. I am telling you not all Soviet citizens are bad guy–type spies who work for the KGB. There are many Soviets who believe Americans and Soviets should be comrades."

"Okay then, what about the goons at the train station yesterday? Who were they?"

"Those men were agents who didn't want me to help you."

Shelby was beginning to see the light, but there was still one other small issue that needed to be addressed.

"What else is wrong, Shelby Hutchinson? Remember, this is the time for truth, yes?"

"Yes," Shelby answered with a long exhalation of breath. "So, Tasha…you almost kissed me. What was that all about?"

Tasha lowered her head and smiled. "That was about you."

"Me? What about me?"

"You are a funny person, Shelby Hutchinson. You have a beautiful smile. You are full of joy and I have never known any other person like you. You also have, how do you say, a fine ass in tight American Levi jeans. So when you were on the floor, I wanted to kiss you. Is it not okay?"

"No, no…it is okay; it just kind of surprised me. I wasn't expecting it."

"Why were you not expecting it? I am not blind. I felt your hands touching me when we were on the motorcycle. I can see you do not always look at my face when you are talking to me."

Tasha stopped long enough to look down at her own T-shirt-covered breasts. "I also felt when you were falling and caught you before. You did not want me to let go. I know this. I can see also that I am right. You have a funny look on your face."

Shelby lowered her gaze to the floor. "It's because I'm afraid."

Tasha gently urged Shelby to raise her head with two fingers under her chin. "You are afraid of many things, Shelby Hutchinson. This I do not understand."

"What's not to understand? My life is boring. I never leave the city where I live. I never do anything but work and go home. Even my best friend thinks I'm boring, and I think it's just because I've never wanted to risk anything." Shelby gave Tasha an exasperated look. "You don't think I'm boring, do you, Tasha?"

"I told you before, you can be anything you want, and you are most definitely not a boring person." Shelby managed a hopeful smile that Tasha returned with one of her own. "You are here, with me, taking large chances, doing crazy things, yes?"

Shelby nodded quickly and gasped when she found Tasha's hands on her hips, pulling her closer. That felt so nice. "Yes, I am here, and that's a great big honkin' yes to the crazy things question, so maybe—"

"Maybe is nothing, Shelby Hutchinson. Everything is here. Everything is now. Tomorrow is tomorrow, but it's not important. Life is too short, so you must worry only about now." Tasha grabbed her wrists and slid them up the door, pinning Shelby to the wooden surface behind her. "Are you afraid of me?"

"Well, sort of. You're kind of a bad girl, what with the motorcycle and the leather jacket and the gun and stuff."

"But, Shelby Hutchinson, you also have a leather jacket and gun. Are you also now a bad girl?"

That stopped her. "Well, I'm not sure. I've just always been such a good girl—"

Tasha pressed her body forward, pinning Shelby completely to the door. "And I believe you also have a bad girl inside you. We must find her for you."

Shelby couldn't answer or even move. She only nodded her agreement. Tasha was right. She gasped as Tasha moved closer to whisper in her ear, "I also think you want a bad girl inside you." Shelby closed her eyes and leaned into the soft touch of fingers trailing down the side of her face. "Do you want that, Shelby Hutchinson?"

"Um…" Shelby didn't have words at the moment. She knew they were there somewhere. They always were, but they were being elusive right now. Maybe they were just nervous. Shelby sure was.

But Tasha was having none of it. She backed off just enough to give her a little room to push Shelby even harder up against the door. Hard enough to rattle the hinges. Hard enough that Shelby knew exactly what was expected, as well as what to expect. Tasha asked again, slower this time, making her intentions clear. "Do you want that, Shelby Hutchinson?"

"Yes."

Shelby wasn't even sure where that particular word had come from, but it was out there now. Did she really want this? Oh yeah, she did, and in a big way. The depth of how badly she wanted to take and be taken, well and truly fucked before returning the favor, was becoming frightening in its intensity. She said it again to make sure Tasha understood it too.

"Yes, Tasha, I want that. I want you inside me, and on top of me, and all over me."

Tasha pushed again, verbally and physically, rattling both the hinges on the door and Shelby's inner bad girl at the same time. "Then show me, Shelby Hutchinson. Show me your bad girl."

Something snapped inside Shelby that moved her to a level of bravery she'd never imagined from herself until this very moment. She yanked her hands free and pushed back on Tasha's shoulders, hard, almost knocking her off balance. Tasha's eyes widened in surprise, just for a second, before a hint of a smile appeared on her face accompanied by a knowing twinkle in her crystal blue eyes. That look only served to deepen Shelby's resolve to have, to take without remorse. Tasha wanted it too. Shelby could feel it in every hyperstimulated nerve ending in her body as she pushed again, sending Tasha reeling backward to land sideways across the bed.

Shelby didn't wait to be invited. She didn't want the invitation anyway. Take and be taken. That's what Shelby's inner bad girl wanted, and she wanted it now. She watched Tasha, who was intently studying her in return as she stood by the side of the bed, then shrugged out of her shoulder holster and hung the weapon from an iron rail on the headboard. She must have hesitated for what Tasha considered to be an inappropriate amount of time, because Tasha grabbed the waist of her pants and dragged her closer to the bed.

"Remember, Shelby Hutchinson, everything is here. Everything is now."

Tasha was sitting on the edge of the bed now, pushing up on the hem of Shelby's tank top. Like a cat, Shelby stretched and arched into the touch of the hands under her shirt, before she peeled it the rest of the way off and tossed it carelessly aside. She twisted her fingers in Tasha's hair as she pulled Tasha closer, encouraging her to suck and lick and bite everywhere she could reach.

Shelby's inner bad girl was fully in charge now as all thoughts of doing the right thing or being boring flew out the window at the same time hands found her ass and squeezed. Shelby reached down and pulled off Tasha's holster. The black T-shirt came off next, followed by a utilitarian white bra. Right before she tossed Tasha's clothing aside, Shelby grinned a little as she thought Victoria's actual Secret probably had nothing to do with being a gun-toting Soviet badass.

It was nice to be able to do something with Tasha's breasts

besides try to sneak a peek at them. Squeezing them together, playing with the nipples, all while Tasha groaned and rolled her head back was definitely a good thing. Almost as good as shoving Tasha back onto the bed to work at the button and zipper on her jeans.

Something sounding very much like a growl reached Shelby's ears when she got tangled up somewhere between Tasha's jeans and her boots. Whether it was her own frustration or Tasha's, Shelby wasn't sure, but she kept plugging away, yanking off the boots and eventually Tasha's black jeans. Tasha sat up again, long enough to hook fingers into Shelby's bright purple sweats, pulling both pants and underwear off with one quick jerk, and yanked her roughly onto the bed. With her own sweats and panties still hanging from her ankles, Shelby struggled to kick off the last of her clothing. The fact that Tasha was sucking on Shelby's fingers didn't help. Neither did the fingers twisted painfully in her hair.

"Everything is here. Everything is now," echoed through Shelby's head like a mantra, and apparently out of her mouth too, though she wasn't aware she had been talking out loud.

"*Da*, Shelby Hutchinson, everything is now." Shelby's fingers were guided insistently toward the place Tasha needed them to be. The pressure on her hand told Shelby exactly what she needed to do, while Tasha's rising hips showed Shelby exactly how hard she needed to do it. She felt wet heat surround her fingers, heard a deep growl of satisfaction, saw Tasha's eyes roll back into her head right before Shelby pulled out to push in again. It seemed to be exactly what Tasha needed, but Shelby couldn't be sure because three fingers inside Tasha seemed to flip some kind of switch, turning off her ability to speak English. Shelby had no idea what the stream of foreign words meant, but she was certain Tasha wasn't ordering a cheeseburger. She was pretty sure it meant something closer to, "Fuck me harder, you crazy American," so that's exactly what Shelby did.

Just when she had decided everything was right, Shelby felt

hands on her shoulders, pushing her roughly onto her back. She heard something else in Russian she couldn't identify, but opted to ignore it in favor of the pressure encouraging her legs farther apart. She officially stopped caring about language when Tasha's fingers slid in, pulled out, and slid in again, harder and faster than the first time. Shelby heard herself growl, felt her own eyes roll back, noted that with each thrust, her own English became reduced to a small collection of phrases, including things like "oh, shit, Tasha" and "harder, please, oh God, fuck me harder."

Tasha understood that. At least Shelby assumed she did when each command to do it harder or faster resulted in exactly what she needed. She felt the telltale tingles start in her legs, but Shelby didn't want to be done yet. There was still unfinished business and Shelby's inner bad girl was determined to finish it first. Collecting her wits enough to push back, Shelby knocked Tasha aside and pulled on her arm, indicating that she wanted Tasha on her stomach. Tasha didn't seem to agree with the decision, but was silenced easily with one or two bites to her neck and shoulder blades. This was Shelby's party now, and she wasn't stopping until she had what she wanted.

And what she wanted was fireworks. Russian fireworks like May Day in Red Square. Shelby growled and bit while she teased with her fingers. She could see the strong muscles in Tasha's back working as her hips came off the bed, giving Shelby all the room she needed to fuck her. It didn't take long, between the teeth-shaped welts all over Tasha's back and Shelby's insistent thrusting, before Tasha was groaning, straining harder to push back against Shelby's hand, and finally, with a long, shuddering growl, coming hard just like Shelby wanted her to.

Shelby was stoked, proud of herself in a way she had never before experienced. The wet, limp pile of naked Russian babe on her bed only made it better. She rolled onto her back to rest, but didn't have long to do so once Tasha collected herself enough to get on her knees and flip Shelby onto her stomach. Turnabout was fair play, after all. It was a little disconcerting being unable to see what was going on, but her anxiety soon disappeared when Tasha found a particularly sensitive spot on Shelby's neck and bit down hard enough that Shelby had no choice but to cry out. It hurt like hell, but in a good way, so Shelby pushed away the urge to struggle and gave in to the growling and the teeth and what felt like Tasha's whole hand in her pussy.

The thrusting was intense, the biting was intense, and when it finally hit, the orgasm was like nothing Shelby had ever known before. She let go with her own version of the long, shuddering growl, clawing for purchase on the covers of the bed, while wave after orgasmic wave crashed over her, threatening to drown her. Finally reduced to something resembling a noodle in her grandma's chicken soup, Shelby had nothing left but to smile the smile of a bad girl set free.

Somewhere in the periphery of her just-been-fucked stupor, Shelby registered the sound of a voice accompanied by strong hands urging her to turn around to get under the sheets and blanket. "Come, Shelby Hutchinson. You must sleep now."

As much as she didn't want the evening to be over, once under the covers, Shelby curled up to enjoy the naked snuggle and realized she was exhausted. "Are you staying tonight?"

Tasha wrapped her arms around Shelby, stroking her hair. "*Da*, I must also sleep. Tomorrow is a big day."

"Why? What's happening tomorrow?"

"Tomorrow we must leave for the Soviet Union, but first, we have to sneak over the border into Poland."

"Sneak into Poland? What? I didn't know…"

"Shh, Shelby Hutchinson, now you need to sleep."

Shelby fought the urge to argue further, because she was almost certain that Tasha wouldn't answer her anyhow. As the anxiety boiled in her gut, Shelby closed her eyes in an attempt to will it down and hoped that sleep would follow soon. She was so tired, but she knew, as she listened to Tasha's deep breathing, that sleep would not come easily.

CHAPTER FIVE

Shelby did eventually fall asleep, but the night had been restless. She wasn't sure what had disturbed her, but she was definitely awake now. She stretched and yawned, noticed it was still dark outside, and rolled onto her back. Ouch. Not a great idea. The collection of sore spots on her neck and shoulders, now emphasized by the slightly rough sheets beneath, served as a vivid reminder of exactly what had transpired last night. Despite her various collections of aches and pains, Shelby smiled. Last night had been intense, definitely something new for the kid from Chicago who always did the right thing.

Shelby felt around the bed and realized she was alone. Not for long, though, as Tasha appeared from the bathroom, toweling off her wet hair. Shelby feigned sleep for a little longer, just to watch Tasha as she wrapped her towel around her torso and tucked it in to keep it in place. She turned to look in the mirror over the dresser while she combed out her long hair and tied it back into a ponytail. Once the hair was out of the way, Shelby's eyes were drawn to the teeth-shaped bruises on Tasha's shoulders. She felt bad about it for a moment, but let it go, her own sore back reminding her that no one had uttered the word "stop" to anyone else. Maybe someone said "don't stop" a time or two, but since Tasha had seemed to lose her ability to speak English, Shelby had no way of knowing exactly what had been said.

Daydreams of last night continued to pop in and out of her head as she watched Tasha get dressed. Shelby gave up faking sleep and sat up, drawing Tasha's attention from the mirror. While she pulled the sheet up to cover her naked breasts, Tasha turned to offer a smile. "Ah, Shelby Hutchinson, you are awake. You sleep like a dead thing."

Shelby laughed a little as she yawned again and scratched her head. "Yeah, I kind of do that."

The mattress shifted as Tasha climbed on and moved up the bed on her knees to give Shelby a kiss good morning. She offered a slightly evil smile. "You also fuck like an animal. I am impressed."

Well, that was a new one. "Um, thank you. I think."

"Oh no, Shelby Hutchinson. It's a good thing." Shelby turned as Tasha gently took her by the shoulder to inspect the damage to Shelby's back. "Oops, I am sorry for the bruises."

"Hey," Shelby answered quickly, "I should be saying that to you. Have you seen your back?"

"*Da*, I saw earlier in bathroom." She took Shelby's hand, urging her to get out of bed. "We must be leaving soon, and you might want to take a shower."

"Yeah, that's probably a good idea." Shelby laughed a little as she tossed aside the covers to get out of bed, then stopped on the way to the bathroom to dig through her duffel bag. She still wasn't sure exactly what was in the bag, besides the large and obvious grenade launcher, but quickly found a small kit filled with personal items. The clothing selection wasn't great, but Shelby didn't care since she had her cool new leather jacket to cover anything she didn't like. After a quick search through the small collection of shirts and underwear, Shelby selected a black tank top to go with her jeans and a pair of blue striped underpants.

On her way into the bathroom, Shelby turned as Tasha offered a warning. "Be careful with the hot water." She got the idea immediately as Tasha pointed toward her own back, reminding Shelby of the damage she hadn't yet seen.

"Oh yeah, thanks." Shelby closed the door of the bathroom and went straight over to the mirror to inspect the bruises on her shoulders. "Yow." She cringed at her own reflection. "And you say I fuck like an animal. Jeez."

Shelby was almost unable to believe all of the changes in only two days. Leather jackets, guns, self-defense workouts, and the most rough-and-tumble sex she had ever experienced. The water pressure wasn't great, but the shower did feel nice. The water quickly started getting cold, forcing Shelby to keep it short. It was probably for the best since Tasha seemed eager to get on the road. Despite her own concerns about what was supposed to happen next, Shelby found she was eager to get going too.

Well, maybe not that eager. There was a huge part of Shelby that wanted to lock the door to the apartment and just stay naked with Tasha for the rest of her stay, but that probably wasn't a great idea. Last night had been lots of fun, but she knew deep down that Tasha, like everything else here in Berlin, was temporary, and there were things that needed to be done. Specifically, prototype grenade launcher kinds of things, and it was time to get moving.

After getting dressed, Shelby pulled the door open. "Tasha, what about breakfast? I'm starving and—" She stopped, seeing that Tasha wasn't the only person waiting for her. "Oh, shit, um, sorry." She pointed toward the stranger. "Who's the big guy?"

The guy was huge and more than a little menacing. Six foot five, maybe six foot six, dark brown eyes, dark brown hair, and another black leather jacket. Shelby couldn't help but wonder if everyone had a leather jacket now.

"Shelby Hutchinson, this is Comrade Boris."

Shelby stopped staring as she remembered her manners and extended her right hand in greeting. "Hi, um, nice to meet you, Boris." He didn't return the attempted handshake, but he did look her up and down before he turned toward Tasha and said something in Russian Shelby didn't understand. Apparently, Tasha didn't like what he had to say, so she fired something angry-sounding back, again in Russian, leaving Shelby in the dark. She felt like a dork standing there with one hand extended, so she made a show of nonchalance, wiping the palm of her hand on her jeans before she remembered her pants were still undone. Make that total dork. She wanted to ask Tasha what the hell was up with him being here, especially the way Tasha had practically thrown her out the window only yesterday, but somehow Shelby knew she would probably get a cryptic answer, so she opted to ignore it for the moment. At least until she had Tasha alone again.

Another quick flurry of Russian from Tasha, and then Boris left. Cryptic answer or no, Shelby wanted to know what was going on.

"Tasha, why was Boris here?"

"Comrade Boris brought information for travel. I told you last night we have to go into Poland with the prototype grenade launcher. It's time to leave."

"Uh, okay. Can't we just drive or get on a train?"

"Ah, Shelby Hutchinson, you still don't understand. We have to get supplies and then we have to sneak you across the border. Poland is a Soviet Bloc state and you are an American with a grenade launcher and a U.S. passport. It's not easy, but we can get on the train in Poland."

Shelby nodded her understanding. Of course she couldn't just walk into Poland, declare the grenade launcher at customs, and be welcomed with open arms. Shelby sighed. "Yeah, okay, I get it." She shrugged into her holster and put her leather jacket on. "All right, I'm ready."

"That is good." Tasha pulled Shelby toward the door and got her moving down the steps. Shelby heard the door close behind her as she trudged down three flights of stairs, more than a little nervous about what was coming next. It didn't help that Tasha was being so silent about their destination. She already knew the trip to Poland would be short, less than fifty kilometers, so Shelby satisfied herself with that knowledge and climbed on the back of Tasha's motorcycle.

The one thing Shelby hadn't remembered was they were still in West Berlin and getting out of town and into the East German countryside wasn't a simple matter. It helped that it was still dark outside. The first glow of a bright red sunrise appeared over her shoulder to the east. Shelby held on as Tasha guided the motorcycle through a series of side streets and alleys and finally stopped in front of an old building Shelby immediately recognized as a bakery. That was good, since Shelby was famished, and the smell of baked goods only made it worse.

She made a beeline toward the door of the bakery, but was stopped when Tasha placed a hand on her chest. "You must keep silent. Say nothing. Do you understand?"

Shelby thought about asking why, but changed her mind. Tasha pushed the door open and went straight to the rather large woman standing behind the counter. It seemed odd here in Germany, but Tasha was speaking Russian to the woman, again leaving Shelby in the dark. After a short conversation, Tasha handed the woman a small black bag, which was quickly hidden under the counter. The woman then pulled a larger backpack out and handed it across the counter to Tasha, who shrugged into the shoulder straps and pulled them tight. She then pulled Shelby behind the counter toward an open door.

Shelby was led down a dimly lit set of rickety wooden steps into the basement of the building. She couldn't help but think she was being led into the bowels of hell as the steps continued down much lower than what Shelby considered normal for your average basement. She felt a knot begin to form in her belly, and it only got worse when she saw where they were headed. A small space with a dirt floor, dimly lit from above by a single bare light bulb and what looked to be a pile of flour sacks stacked against the wall on the far side of the dingy little room. Tasha moved the bags, revealing a small door. Not a normal door, but a simple wooden cover that, once removed, proved to be the entrance to a tunnel.

"What's that?" Shelby asked.

"Shh, Shelby Hutchinson. That is a tunnel to East Berlin."

Shelby's eyes widened. Tunnel? Her anxiety quickly progressed into claustrophobia-induced panic when Tasha pulled out a flashlight and showed Shelby exactly where they were going. She could easily see that this was not a tunnel meant to be walked through. The beam of the flashlight caught and held drips of water in the narrow space, making them sparkle like tiny stars, but it still wasn't enough to keep Shelby from feeling as if she was going to hyperventilate and die. Tunnel. Crawling-through type of extremely small tunnel. Not good.

Shelby was still staring at the small hole in the wall, struggling to breathe, when Tasha handed her the flashlight and pointed toward the space Shelby now knew to be the entrance to hell. Her own personal hell anyway. Despite Tasha's warnings to remain silent, Shelby whispered, "What…me?"

"*Da*, Shelby Hutchinson, you are going first. I must close the door behind us. Is something wrong?"

"No, no." Shelby tried to hide her anxiety from Tasha, but the enormity of it all made the task impossible. "It's just…" She gestured with her hands, indicating she was having trouble with the cramped dimensions of the tunnel.

"Are you afraid of the dark?" Tasha asked quietly, just a hint of a smile quirking at the corner of her mouth.

"No. I'm not afraid of the dark. I'm claustrophobic."

Despite the dim lighting in the small room, Shelby could plainly see Tasha roll her eyes in frustration. She could also see the resolve play across Tasha's face right before she took Shelby by the shoulders and spun her back around toward that tiny little space. With a small shove, Tasha propelled Shelby toward the tunnel. "Now is the time for facing your fear, Shelby Hutchinson. The tunnel is only a short distance. Go."

Shelby swallowed hard. She wasn't getting out of this one. She pulled her duffel over her head, tossed it into the entrance to the tunnel, took a deep breath, and ducked, getting on her hands and knees to begin the crawl into Communist East Berlin. She began moving slowly as she struggled to control her breathing. A mantra began rolling in her head, one she found gave her a modicum of strength.

"I'm facing my fear...facing my fear...oh, shit...I'm facing my fear..."

She was aware of little else besides the duffel in front of her, the damp walls surrounding her, and the occasional hand on her butt from behind that served to keep her moving forward. The one time she tried to look ahead toward the end of the tunnel, it stretched and twisted away from her in an acid-trippy, nauseating kind of way, so she kept her head down and allowed her eyes to travel only as far as the limits of the shaking beam of the flashlight clutched tightly in her right fist. Dampness soaked through the knees of her jeans, and the cold moisture on the uneven rock surface beneath her hands made her shiver. The only sounds she was aware of were the thundering of her racing heart and the occasional hitch in her breathing. After crawling for what felt like an eternity, the duffel fell away in front of her and she tumbled head-first out of the tunnel, only to land roughly in a heap on the dirt floor of a small space similar to the one at the opposite end.

Shelby rolled onto her back and took a long gulp of air. No more tunnel. Woo-hoo. The solitude of her relief was short lived as Tasha climbed out of the tunnel behind her placed a comforting hand on Shelby's shoulder. "Are you okay now?"

Shelby took another long gulp of stale basement air. "Yeah, I'm fine now."

"That is good, Shelby Hutchinson. Welcome to East Berlin. Come quickly. We must keep moving. There is a car outside for us."

They climbed a rickety flight of steps that led to the back of another store. Judging from the assortment of tools and other items on the walls, it was a hardware store, but Shelby didn't have long to think about it as Tasha headed straight for the door and out into the muted light of a gray, depressing morning in Communist East Berlin. The color of the sky seemed appropriate because all Shelby could see as she looked around were gray, depressing concrete buildings, a stark contrast from the bright, urban hustle and bustle of West Berlin.

Tasha dragged Shelby into the alleyway between the hardware store and the building next door. "Come, Shelby Hutchinson. The car is in the alley and we must hurry to cross the border."

Shelby stumbled over her own feet, sloshing through a puddle toward a tiny vehicle shaped like a Kleenex box crafted from fiberglass and rust that she supposed was a car. She reached the passenger side door and pulled on the sticky handle. The door creaked open an inch but slammed out of Shelby's hand, closed by Tasha.

"What are you doing? You cannot ride in the front of the car." She led Shelby to the back of the car where she popped the lid on the trunk and gestured toward the tiny open space in the back. "Since you have only a U.S. passport, you must ride in the trunk until we cross the border."

"In the trunk?" Shelby was incredulous. "You're kidding, right?" She gave Tasha a pleading glance. "Please tell me you're kidding."

"*Nyet*, Shelby Hutchinson. I am not being a funny guy." She gave Shelby another small push toward the trunk. "Get in, please. We must leave now to catch the train in Poland."

"Well, shit." She folded herself into the tight space. Tasha tossed the duffel bag on top of her, and Shelby took a long breath to try to calm down when Tasha slammed the lid of the trunk. The lock didn't catch the first time so Tasha slammed it again, harder. "This should be fun." As the engine of the small car sputtered to life, Shelby couldn't help but think it sounded more like a big lawnmower than an actual car. She also had to wonder if Tasha was hitting every pothole in the street on purpose, but since there was nothing she could do about it, she just closed her eyes to try to keep from freaking out in the small, closed space. The road finally leveled out, leading her to believe they were clear of the city and into the countryside. She knew, because Tasha had told her, the trip to the border would take less than an hour. And as long as the guard at the border didn't decide to be an asshole, Shelby would be out of the trunk and onto a train not long after that.

It turned out that the guard was cool, so twenty minutes later, Shelby was squinting against the light and attempting to wiggle her way out of the trunk. As soon as she was out, Tasha tossed her the duffel bag and headed for the rail platform. Shelby followed Tasha, happy to be free of that deathtrap of a car and headed for a nice, safe train.

Once aboard, Tasha quickly located two seats together. When the train started to move, Shelby gave in to the rhythm of the train and fell asleep.

She was jostled awake sometime later when Tasha got up from her seat and headed toward the ladies' room. Shelby followed Tasha with her eyes until the door to the restroom clicked shut. Two rows forward, a guy who had apparently been waiting for this moment sprang from his seat and came back to sit in Tasha's vacated spot.

"Um, excuse me." Shelby looked over at the stranger. "That seat is taken."

Shelby gasped when she saw a quick flash of the butt end of a semiautomatic handgun as the man reached into his inside jacket pocket and pulled out a wallet. "You're Shelby Hutchinson, right?" He opened the wallet to identify himself as a CIA agent.

"Yeah. Who are you?"

"My name is Riley." He slipped his wallet back into his jacket. "We've been looking for you."

Shelby was shocked. "Looking for me? Why? What did I do?"

"We waited at the hostel on Meininger Strasse. Thought

maybe you missed the train from Frankfurt, but it got later and later and we had no idea where you were. You haven't been easy to track down."

Shelby stared with her mouth hanging open. She had forgotten all about the itinerary that said she was supposed to go somewhere else when Tasha first showed up. "Oh, shit."

"Yeah, oh shit is right. We had no idea what was going on. Thought maybe you were defecting."

"Defecting? No, I'm not defecting, and I don't know what the hell you're talking about. Hey, I still don't know who you are."

"Riley is a bad guy who wants to take things that do not belong to him," Tasha said. Shelby had failed to notice her return. Riley's eyes widened with surprise but he said nothing. Shelby saw that Tasha was holding her Makarov to the back of his neck. Tasha leaned in and whispered, "Let's all take a walk, yes?"

Shelby nodded and she and Riley scooted out of their seats and into the aisle of the train. She could see Tasha was keeping her Makarov close to her body. Tasha motioned with the weapon for Riley to go first, ushering him toward the door at the back of the car. With her free hand, Tasha waved, urging Shelby to stay behind her. Shelby was all kinds of okay with that. She liked having a Russian bodyguard between her and the big guy who seemed to know who she was.

Once they got to the door leading to the space between cars, Tasha said, "Open it," which Riley did, encouraged to do so by the gun held close to his ribs. Shelby stayed back, a little lost in her own confusion. That confusion changed to shock when Tasha raised her Makarov and brought the butt end down hard, impacting Riley's skull with a sickening crunch. He collapsed in a heap as Tasha slid the gun under her leather jacket and back into its holster. She pulled Riley's jacket from his unconscious form and began searching through the pockets. Apparently, she found what she had been looking for, then she tossed the jacket off the side of the moving train. After looking through Riley's identification, she pulled out a handful of cash, stuffed it into her pants pocket, and threw the wallet aside also.

Shelby's shock turned into outright disbelief when Riley started to wake up. Tasha used his own partial consciousness to help him to his feet. His eyes widened in shock and he seemed to know what was coming, but it was too late as Tasha shoved, sending the self-proclaimed CIA agent flailing through the air and off the side of the moving train. Shelby cringed when he hit the ground hard and rolled. "Wow, that's gonna leave a mark," she said as Tasha dusted off her hands, straightened out her jacket, and turned to Shelby.

"Are you okay, Shelby Hutchinson?"

Shelby nodded, still a little surprised by what had just happened. "Yeah, I'm fine. Who was that guy?"

Tasha looked around nervously as she pulled Shelby closer by the open sides of her leather jacket. "Remember when I was telling you there were many people who would try to keep you from your task?" Shelby nodded briskly. "Riley is one of those people."

"But he's an American. He had a CIA wallet-thingy and everything."

"Ah, Shelby Hutchinson, I also have, as you say, a CIA wallet-thingy. It means nothing."

"Well, okay." Shelby wasn't sure it was okay, but she had little choice but to trust what Tasha was telling her. "What happens now?"

"Riley is a double agent, and he never works alone. If he knew about you, then his people also know about you. We must get off the train."

"Off the train?"

"*Da*, off the train. You must head for the front of train. Take the luggage, go to the first car, hide in the bathroom. Wait for me."

Shelby started to protest, but never got the words out as Tasha gave her a shove in the other direction. Shelby made her way toward the front of the train, wrestling with her duffel to keep from inadvertently hitting any other passengers with it on the way. She passed through two cars and into a third, then found the bathroom, slipped in, and locked the door. Soon she heard three small raps on the door and allowed Tasha to squeeze into the small bathroom with her.

"Is everything okay?" Shelby asked.

"*Da*, everything is okay, but Riley's comrade is here. We don't have long until he starts missing Riley."

"That doesn't sound good. Do we still need to get off the train?" Shelby still wasn't greatly enamored of the idea, but she trusted Tasha's judgment. She supposed they could just hide in the station and wait for a later train, so maybe it wasn't so bad.

Tasha nodded. "*Da*, we must get off the train, and we must do it soon." She reached to open the bathroom door. Shelby moved to follow but jumped back when Tasha did the same, closing the door again.

"What's wrong?"

"He is coming up the aisle in the next car." Tasha added a rather terse-sounding Russian word to the end of the statement. Shelby recognized the word from yesterday and immediately decided it meant something close to "oh shit." Tasha looked around the room quickly and seemed to come to a decision. She squeezed past Shelby to open the window, leaned out, and ducked back in quickly. "There is a ladder right outside the window. We must leave that way."

"What?" Shelby couldn't believe her ears. "Climb out the window of a moving train? Are you nuts?"

"*Nyet*, Shelby Hutchinson, I am not nuts. It's better than being shot, yes?"

"Well, yes…"

"So then, you must go."

"Me first? Can't you go first?"

She could see Tasha was getting frustrated again. "*Nyet*, you must go first so I can hand you the luggage and also watch your back. There are no tunnels or big trees. It's mostly farms. You are fine. Now, please go."

"Okay." Shelby took a deep breath and ducked her head under the open edge of the window. The train was moving at a good clip, somewhere in the area of thirty to forty miles per hour. That was Shelby's best guess anyway as she turned to pull herself out the window and took hold of the ladder. She pulled hard to get her feet clear of the window. The wind stung her eyes and whipped her hair as she wrapped her right arm around the ladder and reached back toward the opening to grab her duffel bag. "You are fine, Shelby Hutchinson," she muttered, imitating Tasha's accent as she ducked her head under the strap of her bag. "It's time for facing fear. Well, bite me. This sucks." She started to climb the ladder. Once she got far enough up, Tasha ducked out the window, wiggled into her backpack, and followed, urging Shelby to keep moving with the occasional hand on her butt from below.

Fortunately for Shelby, the ladder curved up and onto the smooth, flat surface of the top of the train, so there was no need for any acrobatic feats. Aside from the occasional vent hood and trap door emergency exit, there was now nothing to hang on to, so Shelby belly-crawled far enough out onto the roof of the car to give Tasha some space to climb on as well. She stayed as low as she could, squinting against the wind as Tasha scrabbled up onto the roof of the train and pointed back, away from the engine, indicating that Shelby should head that way. She managed to crawl to the end of the roof but stopped when she reached the break between the cars. "What now?" she hollered over her shoulder.

"Now you must jump to the next car."

"Oh, no fucking way." Shelby was adamant. Thanks to Riley, she had already seen what happened when the human body flew off a moving train at a moderate speed, and she was in no hurry to try it out herself. But, again, Tasha was having none of it.

"*Da*, Shelby Hutchinson," Tasha shouted over the noise

of the wind. "Remember physics. The train is moving forward. You are moving backwards. You will not fall. It's only a short distance."

Shelby still wasn't sure. "But what about my luggage?"

"Leave the bag. Jump to the next car. I will throw the bag to you."

"Oh, come on." Shelby knew she would have to jump eventually. There just wasn't another option.

Shelby stood with Tasha's assistance, surfing the train with her arms outstretched for balance. She slid tentatively toward the edge and looked down. "Shouldn't have done that," she said as she swallowed the accompanying wash of vertigo. After a long, calming breath, Shelby closed her eyes and jumped. She landed hard on the next car and immediately dropped to her hands and knees. That wasn't so bad. She turned back toward the front of the train and held her arms out, letting Tasha know she could toss over the duffel bag.

Tasha threw the bag then jumped, landing much more confidently than Shelby had. She pointed toward the back of the train again and Shelby got back up on her feet and started moving, each step making her feel just that much more confident that she could do this. She reached the next break between cars and hesitated for just a second. She knew Tasha would probably just give her another push if she waited too long, so she didn't even bother setting down her duffel. With the strap pulled tight around her shoulders, Shelby jumped again, landing on the next car. She managed to stay on her feet this time and didn't even bother to look back. She just kept moving steadily, jumping the break between cars until she got to the end of the train.

Tasha caught up as Shelby crouched low at the end of the train, and she pointed toward the ladder that led down to the landing at the back of the caboose. "That way," Tasha shouted over the noise of the wind.

Shelby dropped to her hands and knees to crawl to the edge

of the car, then began to climb down the ladder. The train chose that moment to lurch to one side, forcing Shelby to grab the ladder even tighter to keep from falling as her feet slipped off and swung free in the same direction as the sway of the train. "Shit, shit, shit." Shelby struggled to maintain her death grip on the ladder and get her feet back onto the closest rung. She managed to regain her footing and wrapped both arms around the metal support rails long enough close her eyes and take a long breath to try to stop the panic she could feel bubbling its way to the surface.

Tasha shouted down from the top of the ladder, "Are you okay?"

"Yeah, yeah. I'm just fucking dandy, thanks." She braved a look skyward and saw Tasha acknowledge her with a nod of her head. Tasha pointed toward the back of the caboose, indicating Shelby needed to get off the ladder and onto the landing. She hung on with one arm as she pulled the duffel over her head and heaved it onto the small platform. It landed with a thud as Shelby adjusted her grip on the ladder to follow. She swung her feet toward the steps and landed hard. She grabbed the rails at the back of the caboose to keep from falling and to pull herself out of the way so Tasha could get off the ladder and join her on the small landing.

"Now what?"

"We must jump to get off the train. Remember to roll when you hit the ground. Okay?"

That was the answer Shelby hadn't wanted to hear. "Okay." She picked up her duffel bag, leaving one hand free for whatever was going to happen next. She didn't get a lot of time to think about it as Tasha took her by the hand, counted to three in Russian, and jumped. Since Shelby didn't have another option, especially considering Tasha was pulling her along, she jumped too. She let go of Tasha's hand and the duffel, windmilling her arms as the train continued forward while Shelby flew to the side. The bag landed with a crunch in the branches of a small bush, followed shortly by Shelby as she hit the ground hard with a grunt and rolled in the deep grass to the side of the rails.

Shelby came to a stop on her back, looked up at the threatening gray sky, and decided she'd had just about enough adventure for one day. She took a quick inventory. Her ankle was a little sore, but after a quick experimental twist of her foot, she decided nothing was broken. Well, nothing but her will.

Tasha's voice sounded in Shelby's ear. "Are you okay, Shelby Hutchinson?"

Shaking like a leaf, Shelby sat up and gave into the meltdown that had been brewing since her first view of the tunnel earlier in the day. "No, Shelby Hutchinson is not okay. Shelby Hutchinson has had it. First you make me crawl through a tunnel with a similar diameter to a toilet paper roll, then you lock me in the trunk of a rattletrap piece of shit car and drive like a maniac through every pothole in East Berlin." Shelby flailed her hands in the air as she continued to rant and rave. "Then, we're on a nice, safe train, but nooo...we can't stay there because there's more spies and goons with guns. So then I get to watch you crack one of them over the head, steal his money, and throw his ass off the train. Great. Just fucking great. But hey, we're not done yet."

Shelby was close to hysterical now. "Next, I get to climb out the bathroom window of a moving train like some crazy person in a silent movie western, where I might just mention I almost fell off because the engineer evidently hates me too, and once I'm safely back on the train, you tell me I have to jump, which I did, and now I'm sitting on the side of the road, God knows where, and there's no fucking way I'm going to ask you what comes next because, honestly, I just don't want to know." Shelby stopped to take a long breath. "So, to answer your question, Tasha, no. Shelby Hutchinson is definitely not okay."

Despite the smile on Tasha's face, Shelby didn't share her good mood. Tasha shrugged. "Could be worse."

Shelby was incredulous. "How? Please tell me how the fuck this could be worse."

"Could be raining."

Meltdown over, Shelby laughed a little and tried to answer, but stopped when she was interrupted by a loud clap of thunder. "Oh, no." Shelby groaned as she looked at Tasha.

Tasha grabbed Shelby's hand and yanked her to her feet as buckets of rain began to fall, whipped by the wind. Shelby snatched her duffel from the bush as Tasha pointed toward a barn about two hundred yards away and pulled again, urging Shelby to make a run for it.

❖

Of all the things Shelby ever imagined doing in her life, this just wasn't on the list. Sitting in the hayloft of a barn somewhere right smack in the middle of Bumfuck, Poland, studying a shaft of moonlight, drinking something Tasha had pulled from her bag and declared to be vodka. Not the most civilized way to drink vodka, that much was for sure. A nice vodka and tonic after work, the occasional ice-cold Grey Goose martini with four olives on the weekend. That was the vodka Shelby was used to.

But there wasn't much left here in Poland Shelby was used to anymore. The crystal clear liquid in the bottle tasted exactly like what she imagined lighter fluid would taste like and was proving to be a little more than mildly intoxicating. Perhaps that's why that shaft of moonlight was so fascinating. Tasha's voice pulled Shelby from her ruminations.

"Shelby Hutchinson, I can tell you are thinking. You have a funny look on your face again." Tasha had just a hint of a slur to her words. She tossed the bottle back toward Shelby. "Here. You must stop thinking and drink more."

Despite her best attempts, Shelby missed the bottle, toppling herself over into the hay. She giggled out a small "oops" and opted to remain right where she was. Anything else just seemed like too much work. "Fuck it."

"Shelby Hutchinson, you are loaded, yes?"

Shelby sat up and attempted to spit out the hay that was stuck to her face. "No...wait, maybe...I think so...lemme check." She stood up and swayed a little. "Um, yeah. Loaded. You?"

Tasha fell back into the hay. "*Da*, I am, how do you say, nailed."

"Hammered. You are hammered." Shelby crawled closer to climb on and straddle Tasha's hips. "But we can talk about nailed if you like."

"What is the difference?"

"Well." Shelby pulled Tasha's T-shirt out of the waistband of her jeans. "Hammered means you're drunk, and nailed, well, nailed means..." Shelby hesitated long enough to work the button open on Tasha's pants, looked around to make sure no one else was listening, even though she knew they were alone, and leaned forward to whisper, "Sex."

"Ah, I understand. It's like when you are being laid."

"Getting laid." Shelby pulled down the zipper on Tasha's jeans. "Screwing, boinking, doin' the wild thing, driving from the backseat, rounding third and heading for home, the horizontal mambo, take your pick. Ooh, roll in the hay. That's a good one. Seems oddly appropriate considering where we are."

"*Da*, Shelby Hutchinson. That seems correct to me also." Tasha held her butt up off the floor so Shelby could remove her jeans. Tasha undid the buttons on Shelby's 501s, encouraging her to lose the pants as well. But Shelby's internal bad girl, totally fueled by her earlier dose of lighter fluid–flavored liquid courage, forged ahead. Pants or no, she didn't care. She just wanted in.

And that's exactly what she did, three fingers deep, using the force of her own hips behind her hand to show Tasha exactly what a good old-fashioned Chicago-style roll in the hay was all about. She rocked and pushed, responding to the pressure of the legs wrapped around her butt. Tasha held on to Shelby's leather jacket, muttering incomprehensible things in Russian that only served to make Shelby rock and push even harder. Tasha's growling might have had something to do with the vodka, but Shelby preferred to think it had more to do with her mad skills, especially when the orgasm hit. She responded with a growl of her own as wet muscles contracted around her fingers and Tasha pulled even harder with her legs, grinding herself against Shelby's hand, still coming hard.

Once the spasms stopped, Shelby pulled out and rolled over, fighting to get her own pants and underwear off over her shoes. She managed to get one leg free. That was good enough, because what she wanted was Tasha's fingers and she wanted them now. Knees on either side of Tasha's hips, Shelby reached for Tasha's hand, letting her know exactly what she needed. Tasha got the point immediately, bracing her hand against her own hip while Shelby climbed on and pushed down. She rocked forward and pulled at the front of Tasha's jacket, urging her to sit up. Tasha let Shelby set the tempo she needed. She drove herself onto Tasha's long fingers, each thrust making her feel like she was going to explode.

At some point, Shelby wasn't even sure when, Tasha pushed her onto her back and really let her have it. She rocked with her hips, mimicking Shelby's earlier actions. Since Shelby only seemed to have two words left, "harder" and "faster," she used them to her best advantage, until finally, with the total lack of modesty vodka often provides, Shelby came with a howl, pulling hard at the pockets of Tasha's jacket to keep her close.

Words filtered through Shelby's inebriated, just-been-fucked moment. "Shelby Hutchinson, you bark like a dog. I like that very much."

"Yeah, Tasha, me too. Woof."

Chapter Six

Shelby came to consciousness slowly, helped along by an odd, scratchy sensation on her cheek. As she experimentally opened one eye just enough to see what was going on, she found herself nose to nose with a rather large, scruffy-looking barn cat. "Oh, shit." Shelby sat up quickly to get away from the attentions of her new feline friend.

Tasha startled awake at Shelby's exclamation, drew her pistol, and almost shouted, "What? What is going on?" Tasha visibly relaxed when Shelby smiled weakly and pointed at the mangy gray cat with the mangled left ear.

"Sorry, Tasha. Mr. Puss here must have thought I was tasty, but I don't think you need to shoot him." Tasha slid her weapon back under her jacket. "He kind of scared me."

Tasha grinned, apparently amused by the whole situation. "Shelby Hutchinson, you are not afraid of a pussycat, are you?"

"No, I'm not afraid of a pussycat. I was asleep, and I woke up and there he was, doing that wet sandpaper tongue thing on my face. Hell, I don't even remember falling asleep." She tried to get up, but realized quickly that maybe she should take it slow. "But I do remember now there was lots of vodka last night." She blinked a couple of times to clear her foggy vision and registered that she also had a sizable headache. It didn't take her long to remember last night had included more than vodka as she looked down and noticed her jeans and underwear were still hanging from just one ankle. "Oops." She felt herself blush and reached for her pants to try to make herself a little more presentable.

Tasha was in a similar state, at least as far as clothing was concerned. Her jeans were in a pile about ten feet away. Since Tasha looked confused about her own state of undress, Shelby pointed toward the knot of denim. "They're over there."

With an understanding nod, Tasha rolled onto her knees and crawled to retrieve her pants. Shelby braved getting up again, this time with a little more success, as she dusted off the hay that was now stuck to her butt and wiggled into her jeans and underpants. She also realized she was definitely in the clutches of a seriously wicked headache. She held her head with both hands and let go of a small groan.

"Ah, Shelby Hutchinson, you are hanging over, yes?"

Shelby forced a smile and laughed a little. "Hung over. Yes, Tasha, Shelby Hutchinson is definitely hung over. Aren't you?"

"*Nyet*, I am not, as you say, hung over. You just need breakfast, then you will again be strong like bull."

Shelby laughed again. "Well, okay. I suppose that is better than being drunk like skunk." She patted her tummy as it growled unhappily. "Maybe I do just need some food. Is there a diner or something nearby?" She had no idea what to think when Tasha threw her head back and howled with laughter. "What? What's so funny?"

"Shelby Hutchinson, we are in, how do you say, the middle of nowhere and Poland is a Soviet Bloc state. There are no restaurants for fifty kilometers."

Well, shit. She hadn't thought of that. "Okay, then what do we do for food?"

"You stay here in the barn. I will go to the house for food."

"To the house? So you know the people who live—" Shelby stopped when she noted the look on Tasha's face. It seemed to warn her not to finish the question. Tasha pulled on her boots and backpack and climbed down the ladder to the lower level of the barn.

Shelby sat next to her duffel bag and began rooting through it for her toothbrush. Her mouth tasted like she'd spent most of last evening chewing on a tennis ball and it was not helping the pain in her head. "Ooh, maybe there's a bottle of aspirin in there too." Shelby smiled when she found what she had been looking for, a bright green plastic bottle filled with white tablets. She climbed down the ladder toward the only source of water she could see, a rain barrel just outside the barn. "Better than nothing, I suppose." She chewed on her toothbrush and shook two tablets out of the small aspirin bottle, which she shoved into a pocket.

She looked up when she heard the back door slam shut and Tasha reappeared from the house. A long loaf of bread was sticking out of Tasha's backpack, but Shelby forgot about it quickly when Tasha began running toward her, waving, and shouting orders. "Go, Shelby Hutchinson, run. Head for the train tracks."

Shelby started to ask what was going on, but she swallowed the question once she saw why Tasha was running. A disheveled man appeared from the back door wearing nothing but boxer shorts, a ratty undershirt, and a pissed-off look on his face. He was shouting something in Polish that Shelby couldn't understand, but she did understand the shotgun held tightly in his large hands. Shelby dropped her aspirin when he cocked the shotgun and Tasha flew right past her, sprinting toward the tracks. The sound of the blast urged Shelby to run like hell. They were both too far away for him to hit them with the shotgun, but Shelby didn't care. She just wanted as much space as possible between her and the business end of that evil-looking weapon, especially considering Tasha had apparently just stolen his food. She ran as hard as she could, clutching her toothbrush in one hand and her duffel in the other, trying to ignore the pain in her head and the sound of the shotgun being cocked again.

They ran until Shelby couldn't run any more. She huffed to a stop, trying to catch her breath and shout to Tasha at the same time. "Wait. I'm done. Can we stop now?"

Tasha stopped running as Shelby dropped her luggage and bent over, hands on her knees. She was still clutching her toothbrush in one fist as she struggled to breathe. Tasha braved one look back toward the farm. "*Da*, we can stop now. Are you okay?"

"Yeah," Shelby wheezed back, "I'm…I'm fine…just need…a minute." She flopped down right next to the train tracks, making a seat out her duffel bag while Tasha dropped her backpack and began to pull out foodstuffs. Shelby watched as bread, a good-sized hunk of some kind of white cheese, something that looked like salami, and a bottle of homemade wine appeared on the ground before her.

Tasha looked up from the picnic breakfast and smiled. "Eat, Shelby Hutchinson. It's good for being hung over."

Shelby warily looked over the assortment of pilfered food. "Is there anything to drink besides wine?"

"Oh, there is still some vodka, if you want it," Tasha said with a smirk.

"Um, no, thanks. Wine is good." Shelby realized there was a problem. "Tasha, you didn't happen to liberate a corkscrew when you grabbed everything else, did you?"

Tasha said nothing. She just picked up the wine and broke off the top by striking the bottle against the steel train track, then she offered it to Shelby.

"Well, that works too." She held out one hand to accept the drink. "I guess I'll give it a go." As Shelby tried to drink around the broken edges of the bottle, Tasha pulled out a knife and began to slice up the meat and cheese. Shelby dug in with gusto.

She ate until she couldn't eat any more. "Better now." She leaned back and patted her full tummy. Then she dug in her pocket for the aspirin bottle, shook out two more tablets, and downed them with a slug of wine.

All that food went a long way toward making Shelby feel better. "Okay, I'm ready. Where are we going?"

Tasha was already walking. "We will go into town to catch the train."

Shelby trotted to catch up. "How far is that?"

"It's not far. Only six or seven kilometers."

Shelby did the math in her head and realized she'd be okay for the three or four miles Tasha was talking about. Since it seemed like a long time to be walking in silence, Shelby attempted to start a conversation. "So, um, Tasha, where are you from?"

"You already know this. I am from the Soviet Union."

"Well, no duh. I know that. I just meant things like, I don't know, what's your hometown? Where did you go to school? Did you have a dog? Whatever. I was just trying to make conversation."

Tasha glanced over her shoulder again, offering Shelby a slightly apologetic expression. "I am sorry, Shelby Hutchinson. Okay, I am from *Moskva*, how do you say, Moscow."

"See, that wasn't so bad. What was it like, you know, where you grew up?"

"It was like what you saw in East Berlin. It was not a big deal." Tasha continued to walk. She seemed to be done talking.

"Well, okay then." Maybe trying to make conversation hadn't been such a great idea. Especially considering Shelby felt like she needed a crowbar to get anything back from Tasha. Maybe she just didn't like talking about herself. Some people were like that. Not Shelby, of course, but she knew one or two.

After a little more than an hour of walking, the train station came into view. Not that hiking along railroad tracks through the Polish countryside with a hot Russian babe was a bad thing, but she was eager to get on with her travels. She couldn't seem to stop thinking about Riley and her forgotten itinerary. The thought niggled at the back of her mind, like an unscratched itch, that she might be walking into an untenable situation, but there wasn't a lot she could do about it now. As she watched Tasha walk up to the ticket window, she came to the decision she was worrying for no reason. It occurred to her that whenever she stared at Tasha's butt, her concerns about spies and their motivations seemed to magically disappear.

Tickets in hand, Tasha turned back toward Shelby. "The trains are slow today. We will have to wait for a little while." She pointed to Shelby's right hand, toward the toothbrush that seemed to have never found its way back to her luggage. "Do you need to brush your teeth? The bathroom is right over there."

Shelby held her hand up and studied the toothbrush. "Um, yeah, I suppose so." She looked down and called herself a spaz as she walked across the platform toward the ladies' room. Two doors at the east end of the building, both with cracked and peeling signs, lettered in an indecipherable script, presented themselves to her. "Well, there's always eeny-meeny-miney-mo." Shelby got as far as catching a tiger by the toe before she decided it didn't matter. She chose the door on the right, held her breath, closed her eyes, and pushed her way gently into the small room. "Hello?"

Shelby opened her eyes. Empty. She found the light switch, flipped it on, and headed for the sink. "Oh, toothpaste would be nice too. I wonder?" She dropped her duffel on the painted concrete floor and began to rummage through the bag for her toothpaste.

The door swung open. Shelby looked up and squinted against the bright eastern sunshine that was partially blocked out by the silhouette of a man. In a trench coat. And a black Fedora. "Oh, shit."

"You have something that belongs to me. Where is the prototype grenade launcher?"

Shelby wasn't anybody's idiot. "What?" She backed away from her luggage and pointed toward it. "This prototype grenade launcher? Take it. It's not mine. I promise. I don't mind. Really...I found it." Shelby rolled her eyes.

"Yuri, please tell her not to try so hard. And tell her to be quiet as well."

Yuri, all six foot two of him, stepped past the guy with the cool hat and drew his Makarov from somewhere deep within his black suit jacket. Shelby couldn't help but notice Yuri's two black eyes and the large hunk of white first aid tape that seemed to be holding his nose to his face. She felt like she should apologize for his injuries, apparently sustained when their tire had exploded and the BMW slammed into the guardrail on the autobahn, but she quickly decided against it. Instead, she slapped a hand over her mouth and waved with the other indicating she was more than willing to do anything Yuri wanted her to do.

Tasha? What the fuck do I do now?

Yuri stepped closer, urging Shelby back toward the wall with a combination of his menacing presence and his Makarov. She banged her head on the paper towel dispenser and stopped flat against the dingy white tile.

The door swung open for a second time. "Shelby Hutchinson, you must stop fooling around. The train is coming, and it's time—" Tasha stopped cold. Everyone froze. Tasha greeted the guy in the hat. "Comrade Sergei Dmitriev."

Fedora Guy nodded back. "Comrade Natasha Mikhaylova. You are looking well."

Tasha shot something back in Russian.

"No, comrade, we will have conversation in English. I want everyone to understand everything I am about to tell you." He gave Tasha a look, which she answered with a nod as he turned his full attention toward Shelby.

"Shelby Hutchinson told me she found the prototype grenade launcher and she would like to give it to me. Is that okay with you, comrade?"

Tasha smiled a little and slid her hands up to her hips. "Comrade Dmitriev, if Shelby Hutchinson said you can take the prototype grenade launcher, then take it." Tasha held her hands out, gesturing toward the duffel bag on the floor. "It's yours. I want you to have it. I do not care either way."

Shelby just stood there and watched. It was intense and she was scared shitless, but Tasha told him to take it, so maybe he might just take it and leave and Shelby could breathe again.

As it turned out, it was over a lot quicker than Shelby imagined possible. As Fedora Guy leaned over to pick up the black duffel bag, Tasha reacted like a flash, pulling her jacket out of the way with her left hand as she drew her Makarov with her right. The gun went off twice and the two goons hit the concrete floor, dead, each neatly shot once in the forehead.

Shelby freaked. "Oh, holy shit, Tasha. Look…wow, look what you did. Oh, jeez, this is bad."

Once again, Tasha was having none of it. "Shelby Hutchinson, all is okay. Grab the luggage. We need to get on the train now or we will have to walk to the Soviet Union."

"But…" Shelby was shocked and struggled to speak as she gestured toward the bodies on the floor. "What about, you know"—Shelby's hysteria began to bubble up—"oh, the, I don't know"—Shelby was almost screaming now—"dead guys in the public bathroom!"

In two quick strides, Tasha had one hand wrapped around Shelby's bicep and the other hand clamped firmly over Shelby's mouth, and the look in her eyes meant business. "Shelby Hutchinson, you must calm yourself. All is okay."

Shelby was starting to calm down, but she still wasn't sure. She reached up to pull Tasha's hand away from her mouth. "But, Tasha, what about the bodies?"

"You and I need to be on the train. Take the luggage, go out the door, and wait for me. I will lock the door and go out the window. The train will leave and we will be gone to the Soviet Union. You must do this now."

Shelby didn't say anything. It wouldn't have mattered anyway. She just nodded, squeezed past Tasha, picked up her duffel, and walked out the door. The lock clicked behind her. She turned to catch the backpack as Tasha handed it out the window and then followed right behind. Once the window was closed, Tasha reclaimed her backpack and started walking toward the train. Shelby still didn't have much to say. Surprisingly, it was Tasha who broke the silence.

"Shelby Hutchinson, did you really tell Comrade Dmitriev you found the prototype grenade launcher?"

Shelby laughed at Tasha's question. "Yes, Tasha, I did. Some badass courier I turn out to be."

"You are fine, Shelby Hutchinson. You can get on the train and then fall asleep like you always do when we are on the train, and when you wake up, we will be in the Soviet Union, and the scary work will be over."

Considering what had just happened in the bathroom, coupled with everything else, that sounded like a good idea to Shelby. This was all starting to get a little scary. Oh, and there was that niggling little itch at the back of her mind that just wouldn't seem to go away. Maybe Riley had been right. Maybe she should have listened and gone with him. Shelby was getting extremely worried.

Try as she might, once they were aboard and the train got to cruising speed, Shelby couldn't stay awake. She tried to amuse herself with enhanced imaginings of a vodka-fueled roll in the hay, but the rhythm of the rails and her fatigue were just too great to overcome.

Tasha nudged her with an elbow, waking her up. "Shelby Hutchinson, we are here."

"Cool. Wow, it's still dark outside."

"*Da*, it's early morning." Tasha checked her watch. "It's only three thirty."

Shelby yawned and scratched her head. "Did I just sleep for almost twelve hours?" Tasha nodded.

"You had a busy few days. You are tired. It's okay, Shelby Hutchinson. There are friends who will meet us at station."

Shelby silently agreed. She was so tired.

The train hissed and rattled to a stop. Tasha made for the door while Shelby pulled her duffel from the overhead bin and followed Tasha off the train. The train sat for a couple of minutes, then the engineer blew the horn, and the train pulled out toward Moscow and other points east.

It didn't take Shelby long to notice that she and Tasha were the only people who got off the train. It was easy to see when Tasha's people showed up. Boris was a familiar face, but Shelby didn't know who the guy was in the cheesy pinstriped suit, which was fine because she was sure she didn't like him. There was something about him. It took a moment for Shelby to find the right word. Sinister. Yeah, that was it. This guy was sinister.

As Shelby looked around, she came to the realization this whole setup struck her as being a little on the sinister side as well. Dark railroad sidings in the middle of the night, steam from the train hanging in the chilly air. "Kind of creepy." Shelby rubbed her arms, shuddered, and returned her attention to the three comrades now gathered. "Yeah, but if you want to talk about creepy, it's this bunch." A raucous conversation broke out between Tasha and the two men, in Russian, of course, so Shelby couldn't understand a word of it. "Well, that just figures, doesn't it? Seems friendly enough. Friends hanging out, catching up…wait." It became apparent from all the finger poking and shoulder punching that the men were teasing Tasha about something. "Wonder what she did that they think is so funny." It didn't take her long to figure it out. "Oh my God, these assholes are talking about me!" She didn't understand the words, but she understood the gestures and their accompanying sexual innuendo. "Hey now, that's just rude." Tasha said nothing in response to their taunts, but Shelby saw the evil little half-smile when it broke out on Tasha's face, betraying the truth to everyone present. "You, you, you…bitch. You did not just go there." The men broke into gales of laughter, pounding Tasha on the back, offering what Shelby could plainly see were offers of congratulations, apparently because Tasha had managed to bag herself a gullible American. "Yep, I guess you did go there. Bitch."

Shelby could only stare with her mouth hanging open. It got more surreal when Tasha came close to Shelby and pulled at her duffel, guiding the strap over Shelby's head. Shelby got nothing from Tasha. No reassuring smile, no "thanks for the help," no "kiss my ass," nothing. "It's as if I'm not even here," Shelby thought. Tasha turned away and dropped the bag, pulled out the prototype grenade launcher, and tossed it toward Mr. Cheesy Pinstripe Suit. Shelby watched, even more puzzled, when he caught it and responded by pulling a large wad of cash from his pocket and tossing it back toward Tasha. She caught it with both hands, peeled off about a quarter of the roll of bills, handed it to Boris, and stuffed the remainder in the pocket of her leather jacket. Shelby still didn't understand what was going on when Tasha turned back toward her. She didn't seem to be interested in sharing her finder's fee or whatever the heck the money was for. In fact, Tasha didn't seem to be interested in much of anything about Shelby anymore.

"So, Tasha. Does this mean we're done? I can go back to Chicago and you can go rape and pillage your way through half of Eastern Europe, or whatever it is you and the rest of your Klingon shipmates here cook up? Is there anything else?"

Tasha turned to leave. It appeared as though she was going to walk away, but she stopped, turned back, and held up her right hand in a gesture that looked like she'd just remembered something forgotten at the grocery store. "*Da*, Shelby Hutchinson, there is one last thing."

Shelby shifted her weight and crossed her arms over her chest. "What is that, Tasha?"

Tasha crossed her arms, mirroring Shelby's pose. "You never belonged here. This is not your world." Tasha shook her head and stared at the ground. "It's too bad, really."

Once Tasha reached for her Makarov, Shelby froze. Tasha

brought it to bear and pointed straight at Shelby's face. Shelby threw up her hands as if to block whatever was coming. It was already too late. There was nothing she could do but shout, "Tasha, NO!"

"*Do svidaniya*, Shelby Hutchinson."

Shelby saw and heard everything. Tasha's finger as it squeezed the trigger, the flash from the muzzle, the sharp crack of the blast. Then nothing.

CHAPTER SEVEN

S helby's eyes snapped open and she freaked. "What the? Where the? How the? Why?"

She was fully awake now and confused as hell. It was dark. Pitch black, in fact. Shelby reached up to touch a spot on her forehead just above her left eye. It hurt. To be precise, it hurt like hell. Her fingers never made it all the way to her face. They stopped, forward progress impeded by something on her head. Something that felt like a helmet, maybe a motorcycle helmet.

Shelby gasped as realization dawned. "No, doofus. Virtual reality helmet. This is Head Trip. I'm in Chicago." She tried to sit up, but there was too much electronic rigging tethering her to the large black technological marvel of a recliner. "And I'm alive."

But Shelby quickly discovered she was something more than relieved. Shelby was pissed. Pissed in a way she had never before experienced in all of her twenty-seven years.

"That bitch," Shelby said softly. "That motherfucking bitch."

Shelby jumped a little when she heard a door slam open and feet pounding their way closer to where she was sitting. A concerned-sounding voice materialized right next to Shelby. She recognized the voice. It was Andrew.

"Ms. Hutchinson. Are you all right? You're not supposed to be back yet."

"Yeah…right…I'm fine…whatever. Please get me out of this chair." She squirmed in her seat.

"Oh, okay," Andrew answered nervously while he attempted to explain. "Your vitals went nuts, so much so that it bumped you out of the construct. What happened?"

Shelby relaxed and began to breathe a little easier once Andrew disconnected the wires and helped her to remove the helmet. She swung her feet over the side of the chair and scratched her head vigorously with both hands. "She shot me. Execution-style." Shelby made a gun shape with her left hand and pointed to the sore spot just over her eye. "Right here."

"Who shot you?" Andrew asked, tilting his head.

"Tasha shot me."

"Tasha?" Andrew rubbed idly at his chin. "Oh, Natasha. The bad guy."

"Bad guy? Tasha was the bad guy? Well, shit."

Andrew didn't answer. He held up a finger to indicate she should wait. He trotted over to a nearby desk, picked up a file folder, pulled out a single sheet of paper, and began to read it aloud. "Okay, here she is. Comrade Natasha Mikhaylova." Andrew looked up with an expression Shelby couldn't quite make out. "Oh, yeah. She's bad news. Let's see here…" Andrew returned his attention to the computer printout. "Born January, 1957, in Moscow, so twenty-eight years old in your construct. Ex–Red Army commando and sharpshooter, ex-KGB operative, assassin for hire, rogue mercenary, wanted by Scotland Yard, the CIA, the KGB, and, well, just about everybody else."

Shelby had to see for herself. Andrew squeaked and flinched a little when she snatched the printout from his hands. After a quick scan, she found the information she had been looking for. "Wanted for crimes ranging from shoplifting to extortion and murder. Deep-cover secret government operations. Terrorism. Jeez, Tasha."

"She was supposed to be your adversary, Ms. Hutchinson."

"Adversary?" In addition to being pissed, Shelby was

beginning to feel stupid. "And I was her rube. I'm such an idiot. I fell for all of it. Hook, line, and sinker." She could only sit and shake her head while she read the rest of it. She should have gone to the hostel and met Riley. Tasha was supposed to have been the distraction, the James Bond–style bad girl, definitely not someone to be trusted. Well, Shelby had been foolish enough to trust her, and look what happened. "Stupid, stupid, stupid." She crumpled the paper and hurled it past Andrew toward the other side of the room.

But Andrew apparently wasn't ready to let it go. "Ms. Hutchinson, maybe you should have let me explain. I could have told you—" Andrew stopped, mid-sentence, when Shelby gave him her best don't-you-dare-fucking-finish-that-sentence face. It seemed to work.

"I need to get out of here. I need to go home." Shelby was done.

"But, Ms. Hutchinson, you still have three days of vacation coming to you. I can hook you back in and you can go to a nice beach or something…"

"I just want to go home."

"I can give you a credit on a gift card."

"Fine." Shelby pushed herself to her feet. She was a little unsteady but waved aside Andrew's offers of assistance. "I'm okay. It was just a small-caliber penetrating head wound sustained from point-blank range." She gave him two thumbs up and an artificially bright smile. "We're good. Just point me toward the locker room so I can get my stuff and get out of here."

"Of course." He pointed in the general direction of Shelby's belongings and scurried away to get her gift card.

Shelby dressed quickly, grinning a little to herself as she buttoned up her old favorite jeans. They were loose and comfortable, and that was a good thing. What the hell had they been thinking in 1985? She grabbed her backpack from the locker, tossed her scrubs in the provided hamper, and pulled the door open to go settle things with Andrew.

He welcomed her back, offering her a seat opposite him at a small desk. "Here's your gift card." He slid an envelope across the surface. "That's good anytime. Just give us forty-eight hours' notice if you want to use it so we can program your construct." Shelby nodded. "Do you have any questions or concerns? Anything about the experience you found to be troubling or problematic?"

"Besides the part where some random badass Russian babe makes me her bitch?" Shelby shook her head. "No, I'm clear on all of it. Well, there is one thing, when I woke up, my head hurt like hell where, you know…" Shelby gestured toward her forehead. "It still hurts a little. Is that normal? Will it go away?"

"Oh, Ms. Hutchinson. There's nothing to worry about." Andrew smiled warmly. "Sometimes, especially when…well, when something bad happens and you get drawn out of the construct, other clients have complained the experience had been jarring and there was occasionally a phantom kind of pain, but they all reported they were fine and back to normal within the first twenty-four hours. Just take a couple of Advil if it gets worse and give us a call. You'll be fine too, I assure you." Andrew smiled again. "But if you have any problems at all, please contact us right away."

She couldn't help but think he sounded a little bit like a used car salesman. There was one more small problem and Shelby was hesitant to bring it up. "Can I get a copy of the printout for my trip? Sorry about the, you know, freaking out and throwing it at you thing back there."

"No problem at all." He leaned across the desk and offered her a conspiratorial whisper. "You're not the only person who's ever done that, so don't feel bad. I'll get you a data copy on a thumb drive too, then I'll be right back and you can be on your way."

Shelby breathed out a long sigh of relief, happy with the thought she could leave soon. She felt a strong urge to be outside, but not outside on a dark rail platform in the middle of the night.

Shelby was definitely done with that scenario. Andrew soon returned with a large envelope for her. They shook hands and she headed out the door and into the hallway.

Shelby opted to blow off the elevator in favor of the steps and once outside, she breathed a sigh of relief. "Ah, Chicago. Home sweet home...*brrr.*" She shivered and pulled the zipper of her puffy green ski jacket up to her chin, all the while fighting the urge to spread her arms wide and spin on the sidewalk. It was good to be home.

So good, in fact, Shelby felt like walking around downtown, maybe taking the long way home. Her vacation wasn't supposed to end until early this evening, but hey, sometimes getting shot in the head can force a change of plans. Somehow, that thought didn't make her feel better.

Since it was only noon, Shelby decided to walk down North Halsted Street, with all its funky cool places to shop. Not that she'd ever bought anything there. Shelby tended a little more toward the pragmatic when it came to things like shopping for clothes, but that was not the case today. She stopped dead in her tracks in front of the funkiest vintage clothing store she'd ever seen. There it sat in the front window, and Shelby swore she could hear it calling out to her. A black leather bomber jacket.

Go in, Shelby Hutchinson. Put on the jacket. It will make you look like an American tough guy.

"Cool," Shelby said with a smile as she pushed gently on the door and stepped inside.

Afternoon faded into evening while Shelby stared at her computer. Camped out on her sofa, elbows on her knees, laptop on the well-worn surface of the coffee table, Shelby stared at the screen. At the black-and-white digital image. At the dossier that was at some points frightening, but Shelby still felt compelled to read. Every word of it. Several times.

She cocked her head and leaned forward to address the picture on the screen. "I trusted you. What did you do to me?" Despite her best hopes, Shelby didn't figure she'd get much of an answer.

With a frustrated huff, Shelby sank back into the worn cushions of her ratty sofa. She pulled her new leather jacket tighter around herself and idly rubbed at the left side of her forehead. It still hurt. She hoped Andrew had been right about it fading over time. "It'll be fine in the morning." Shelby comforted herself as she flopped onto her side and stretched out her legs on the sofa. Within minutes, she was asleep.

CHAPTER EIGHT

After a fitful night spent tossing on the sofa, Shelby startled awake when the alarm went off on her cell phone. She slapped at the coffee table, blindly searching for the damn thing. It was still dark outside, but Shelby reminded herself it was Chicago and it was January and it was also time to get ready for work. Shelby hauled herself off the sofa and stumbled into the bathroom. She was still tired, but she was also notoriously not a morning person.

Ah, Shelby Hutchinson, you sleep like a dead thing.

She snapped on the light in the bathroom and squinted at her reflection in the mirror. "Yeah, yeah, I know. I also fuck like an animal," she muttered in her best phony Russian accent. "Whatever."

She was halfway to the train before she realized she had once again forgotten to wear a hat. She ruffled her hair and allowed her fingers to trail down to her forehead. It was still sore. Shelby leaned her head against the cool glass of the train window and took inventory. While her head didn't hurt as much as it had yesterday, she was tired. "I suppose getting shot in the head might do that. It'll be fine." She stared at the commuters on her train, lost in their own concerns, and kept coming back to her own. It was an effort to lift her head from the frosty window.

"Maybe I should call Andrew. Or maybe I should just stop being such a pussy."

Shelby walked the five blocks to the hospital, then up to the Information Systems Department. Same old white walls, same old doorways, no spies or double agents or duffel bags loaded with weapons of mass destruction.

The elevator stopped on the fifth floor, just like it always did, and Shelby stepped off and turned down the long hallway leading to her office. Jake was already here. She could hear him checking the messages from the night shift. He didn't even look up from his notes when she poked her head in the door of his office. "Mornin', Shel."

"Mornin', Jake. How was the weekend?"

"Ah, you know. Stuff and things." Jake's expression brightened. "Ooh, tell me about your trip. Was it cool? What happened? Did you shoot lots of badass commies?"

"Buddy, I've got stories about badass commies enough to amuse you for days. But not before coffee. No way." She headed for the comfort of her own office. Jake was hot on her heels. He beat her to the coffee and poured her a cup. "New jacket, Shel? Very retro."

"You like it?" Shelby modeled a little so he could check it out.

"Yeah, sure. Is that what all the hip kids were sporting in 1985?" He handed Shelby her coffee and flopped into his usual place in the chair across from her desk.

"Not the hip kids, so to speak, but the black leather jacket is apparently the uniform for every badass secret agent type that ever plundered and thieved their way though Eastern Europe." She gave Jake a weak smile. "I kind of had one too, and I liked it, so when I was on my way home Sunday afternoon, there was this shop—"

"Whoa, brake lights. Back it up. You said Sunday afternoon. You were supposed to be cyber-tripping until Sunday night. What's with that?"

"That's a loaded question and will require a very long answer. Let's just say my little trip didn't go exactly according to plan."

"According to plan? They were supposed to give you all these instructions and stuff. Did you lose them or something?"

"Worse."

"Worse?"

"Yeah, worse. I didn't let the vacation guy give me all the details before I left." Shelby bit her lower lip. "I kind of fucked up, things got weird, and I got done early."

"What do you mean, things got weird?"

"I mean right off the bat, I got mistakenly hooked up with the badass villain babe instead of the good guys. She totally suckered me in. But, a little in my own defense, you should have seen her butt."

"Fine?"

"Oh, yeah. She had these black jeans and, well, never mind." Shelby steered the story back to the relevant part. "But she was also one smooth operator. She said she was there to help me, and then all this stuff happened, and it turned out I was nothing but a means to an end for her."

"Stuff happened? What kind of stuff?" He stopped talking as realization dawned. "Shel! Did you get laid?"

"Jake!" Shelby tried to look offended, but it just wasn't working. Instead, she gave him an evil little grin, held up two fingers, and waggled her eyebrows.

"Shelby Hutchinson, you're a dog."

"Yeah, buddy, I've heard that before too."

Shelby Hutchinson, you bark like a dog.

"Shel, are you okay?"

Shelby felt funny. "Um, yeah. I'm good." She felt really funny. And her head was beginning to throb. "I'll be fine." She reached up to her forehead.

"Are you sure?" Jake asked. "You have a funny look on your face. Maybe you should sit down."

"What?" Shelby's head hurt. It hurt a lot. "Ow. Jake?"

"Shel!"

She didn't answer. Everything got gray and fuzzy. She felt her eyes roll back right before the floor rushed up to smack her in the face. Then everything went black.

CHAPTER NINE

S helby's eyes snapped open.
"Tasha...no!"

Her hand flew to the painful spot on the left side of her forehead. "Oh, shit, she shot me." Panic-stricken, Shelby panted, breath coming hard in short bursts as she checked her hand for the blood she felt certain would be there. "What the fuck?" No blood. "But she shot me...I don't..." Her heart continued to race as her eyes darted from side to side. "Where...what?"

"Shel?" A male voice. Shelby didn't recognize it.

"Who are you?" Shelby was terrified. "Where is Tasha? Did you see what she did?"

The guy looked scared, as he got up from his chair in the corner and approached tentatively. "Shel...it's me...Jake. Who is Tasha?"

"Jake?" Shelby tried to sit up. A tidal wave of vertigo washed over her. She fell back onto the bed and closed her eyes in an attempt to stop the spinning and the confusion.

"Shel, you're in the emergency room."

"Emergency room? Where?"

"Chicago." She felt strong hands wrap around her upper arms. "You're in the ER at Northwestern Memorial. Work, remember?"

"Northwestern Memorial? Work?" She knew this guy.

Familiar brown eyes. Puzzled expression on his face. She knew this place. The white tile walls seemed familiar. She could hear the hum of machinery, punctuated by the occasional electronic beep, and muted bits of conversation. And the disinfectant smell. She recognized that too. "What happened?"

"You had a seizure. You don't remember anything?"

Shelby shrugged.

"We were talking. You were telling me about your trip. And then you said 'ow,' grabbed your head, and boom, down you went."

"Just like that?" Shelby didn't remember any of it.

"Just like that." Jake offered her a small smile. "You scared the shit out of me."

"I'm sorry. I didn't mean—"

"Forget about it. Do you feel better now?"

"I feel like somebody tried to blow my brains out." Without thinking, Shelby gently touched the spot over her left eye with her fingertips.

"Tasha?" he said.

Shelby panicked, gripped the rails of the bed, and tried to get up again. "Tasha! What? Is she here?"

Jake clamped down on her arms, pinning her back to the bed while she struggled to get up. "No, Shel. Take it easy. No one's here. Who is Tasha?"

She breathed a little easier hearing Jake's reassurance and quit struggling enough that he let go of her arms. "Tasha? She's the Russian babe. You know...fine ass...shot me in the head."

"Shel? What happened? Besides the shot you in the head business. I get that part. Is that why your vacation ended early?"

It was all coming back to her now. "Yes, my vacation ended early because Tasha shot me. Well, come to think of it, she executed me, but why quibble about words?"

"Quibble? Executed? What did you do?"

"I didn't do anything, Jake. I just didn't—" The door opened and a man in a white coat stepped into the room.

"Ms. Hutchinson? Are we feeling better now?"

"We? Not sure about we. I feel like death warmed over." She looked up to meet the doctor's eyes. "Sorry."

"No, no, Ms. Hutchinson. I understand. Does your head still hurt?"

Shelby nodded.

"Still dizzy? Nauseous? A little disoriented?"

Shelby nodded to all of the above.

"Any injuries lately? Head trauma? Anything like that?"

Shelby began to tell the tale of her Head Trip vacation, the shooting, and the rude awakening when it was over. The doctor reacted to the story, nodding appropriately, looking concerned and making a note or two on Shelby's hospital chart.

"I've read a little about these virtual experiences, and everything seems to indicate they're safe enough, but just to be cautious, I'd like to order some tests."

"Tests? What kind of tests?"

"Oh, nothing invasive. Tomographic brain scan, blood test, an external stimuli test to check for epilepsy."

"Epilepsy?" Shelby felt the anxiety begin to bubble again. She forced it down and reluctantly agreed to the tests. "Sure. When?"

"I think it would be best to do it right now. I'll go have the charge nurse make the arrangements and we'll get you up and out of here as soon as possible."

That all sounded like a great plan, but Shelby didn't want to do it alone. "Jake? Would you hang with me while they do all this stuff?"

"Sure thing. I'll call upstairs and check in, then I'm all yours. Okay?"

"Yeah, that sounds great." She reached out to squeeze his hand. "Thank you."

❖

Almost eight hours later, Shelby was leaning against the open door of her apartment, trying to convince Jake she would be perfectly fine home alone.

"I have to, Jake. You know? Besides, this is what I do every night. And, hey, I have this cool hospital microchip telemetry thingy if I have another seizure." She idly scratched at the spot on her scalp where the doctor had injected the tiny device. "If anything serious happens, the hospital will call me, and if I don't answer, the EMTs will be here in less than five minutes. I'll be fine."

"But the doctor said that you shouldn't be alone. Remember? You even told them you had someone that could stay with you. Otherwise, they wouldn't have let you come home."

"Jake," Shelby pleaded, "I just couldn't stay there. You know? Between the Head Trip and last night on the sofa, I just needed some quality time in my own bed."

"Yeah, I know. I just worry about you is all."

"Well, don't worry all night. I'm just going to put on my sweats, get into bed, surf online, and watch TV. I'm fine, I promise."

"Okay. But if you need anything…"

"Yes, I have my phone. Now, before that shot they gave me totally kicks my ass, I'm going to bed." She looked up to meet his eyes. "Thank you, Jake."

He left and Shelby pushed the door closed, leaning against it until the deadbolt clicked. What a long, strange day it had been. A battery of tests followed by the completely anticlimactic diagnosis that there was nothing there. No shadows, no spots, no epilepsy…nothing. Just a phantom pain from a shooting that, in reality, never happened.

Shelby headed into the kitchen to get a Coke and to see if she had any crackers.

You must eat, Shelby Hutchinson.

"Fuck you, Tasha," Shelby said into the air of her empty kitchen. "This is all your fault."

How is this my fault?

Shelby closed her eyes and leaned back against the kitchen counter, wrapping her fingers around the cool stainless steel of the sink for support. "This is your fault, Tasha, because I trusted you. I trusted you and you fucked me over."

But I was not the only one. You were not exactly truthful with me.

"Yeah, yeah, I know." Shelby turned on her best Russian accent, laced with a big dose of sarcasm. "We must find inner bad girl for you, Shelby Hutchinson." She took a can of Coke from the fridge, held the cold aluminum against her phantom head wound, and shuffled into the bedroom.

CHAPTER TEN

S helby sat bolt upright in bed and shouted, "Tasha, no!" Her heart was racing, she was gasping for air, and she was certain when she removed her hand from the sore spot on her forehead, it would be covered with blood. But it wasn't. "What the—?"

She shaded her eyes with one hand, squinting against the bright light filtering in through the slats of the vertical blinds, and made a visual scan of the room. Her eyes were drawn to a pizza box–sized chunk of white cardboard, propped in a chair where it would have been difficult to miss. It was a simple note, hand-lettered in DayGlo pink permanent marker, large enough to see from anywhere in the room:

Chicago
January, 2039

"Oh, shit, not again." Shelby reached up to hold her head with both hands, closed her eyes, and fell back onto the bed with her head on the pillow. The sign was a project from earlier in the day. It had seemed like a good idea, and was proving to be quite helpful in reminding her she had just had another seizure and the pain in her head was, in reality, nothing. Just the thought of that pissed her off all over again. She found her phone on the floor next to her nightstand and called the hospital before they called her, just to get the conversation over with. "Yes, I'm fine. No, I don't need an ambulance." Same conversation every time, and Shelby was becoming more than a little annoyed by the whole process. Maybe it was time to call Andrew at Head Trip. She thumbed though the call log on her phone until she found his number.

After two rings, he answered. "Good morning, Head Trip Travel Services."

She closed her eyes against the pain and the light. "Andrew, hi, this is Shelby Hutchinson. Remember me from over the weekend?"

"Yes, Ms. Hutchinson, I do. Is there something I can do for you?"

"Yeah, actually I was calling to ask you about my trip. I still have that headache that you said would go away in a day or two, and now it's escalated into seizures."

"I'm so sorry to hear that. Have you sought medical attention?"

"I have. The doctors at Northwestern Memorial tell me that there's nothing wrong." Shelby experimentally opened one eye. Bad idea. She pulled the sheet over her face to block the light. "I'm sure you can imagine that I'm more than a little concerned here."

"I'd like to assure you again, Ms. Hutchinson, that you will be fine. Your issues should resolve within the next day or so, but if you need to, please have your doctor call me. I will be happy to answer any questions that he or she might have. We only have your best interest in mind and—"

Shelby couldn't listen to this again. Her head hurt too much, so she cut him off. "Okay, then thanks." She snapped her phone closed. "Asshole." He still sounded like a used car salesman, so Shelby got disgusted all over again. With a frustrated grunt, she extricated herself from the tangled mess of sheets on the bed and shuffled her way into the bathroom. She met her own reflection in the mirror, complete with its dark circles under the eyes and the wildest case of bed hair she had ever seen. "Wow, I look like shit." She poked at her forehead. Although she really didn't think it would help, Shelby turned on the faucet, splashed some cold water on her face, and looked back, dripping wet, into the mirror. "I was right. It didn't help." She lightly touched the spot immediately above her left eye. "Ow."

Shelby scuffed her way back through the bedroom and out into the kitchen, ranting sarcastically to herself the whole time. "They all reported they were fine and back to normal within the first twenty-four hours. Well, that's just crap, Andrew. It's been"—she hesitated to look at the clock on the microwave— "wow, it's been seventy-two hours, and I'm neither fine nor back to normal." She reached into the refrigerator to grab another Coke and lifted the cold aluminum can to the sore spot on her forehead in an attempt to find some relief. Fortunately, her head didn't hurt all the time; only right before or after a seizure, and the combination of cold Coke cans and Advil seemed to manage it pretty well. She opted not to take the pain medication provided by the hospital because it made her feel dopey and a little sick to her stomach.

Shelby Hutchinson, you are loaded, yes?

"Tasha, please, not now. I just got out of bed," Shelby warned the empty kitchen. She turned to reach over the sink for a couple of Advil, downed them with a handful of water from the faucet, and stayed right where she was, elbows on the edge of the sink, Coke can on her forehead, trying to decide what to do next.

"So calling Andrew is apparently a waste of time." Shelby had called him Monday night when she got home from the ER and had, once again, been assured she would be fine. Now it was Wednesday, it was close to noon, and she now had proof Andrew was just as full of shit as he had been on Monday. The doctors at Northwestern Memorial had also been full of assurances she would be fine, but she couldn't help but think their supportive words had been more for themselves than for her. She knew full well there were very few doctors who would admit they were clueless and there was nothing they could do.

Shelby startled to the sound of a knock at her front door. She hauled herself away from the sink and over to the video monitor for the hallway. One push of a button revealed her caller to be Jake, and from the appearance of the bag in his right hand, it looked like he was bringing lunch. She opened the door.

"Hey, Jake." She tried to sound cheerful, but it just wasn't working.

"Hey, Shel. Wow, you look—"

"Yeah, yeah, I know. I look like shit." She held her Coke can up for him to see. "It's the red. It's just not my color. Come on in. It's been a rough couple of days."

He gave her a long, comforting hug. "We've missed you at work. Everyone says hey and all that." Shelby nodded as he held a white paper sack up for her to see. "I brought lunch. Are you hungry?"

"Eh, you know. Sometimes…" Shelby hesitated. She was tired of listening to her own complaints and figured Jake probably needed a break too. "Sorry, Jake. Yes, I am hungry. Thank you."

"You're welcome." He set the bag of food on the counter. "Do you want to eat it or just hold it up against your face?"

"Depends on what it is," she said, offering him a little sarcasm in return.

"Hey, nothing but your favorite. Pho noodles from that grubby little Vietnamese place you love so much."

"Ooh, good choice." He pulled containers of noodle soup and chopsticks out of the bag. "There's more Coke in the fridge if you want one."

Drink in one hand, soup in the other, Jake followed her into the living room and claimed his usual spot in the beat-up chair next to the coffee table while Shelby set down her soup and flopped onto the couch.

"Is this her?" Jake asked as he pointed to the Head Trip printout Shelby had left lying on the coffee table.

"Yeah, that's her." Shelby wasn't certain she was ready to have the Tasha conversation with Jake yet.

"She's definitely hot." Jake always had a way of cutting to the relevant parts.

"Yes, sir, that she is…I mean was…whatever."

This is the time for facing fear, Shelby Hutchinson.

"Yeah, yeah, I know."

"You know what, Shel?"

Shelby closed her eyes when she realized she had spoken out loud. "What? I didn't say anything."

"Yes, you did. You said 'yeah, yeah, I know' and I didn't ask you a yeah-yeah-I-know kind of question."

"This is going to sound incredibly stupid." She looked up to see how he had reacted. "It was Tasha."

"This Tasha?" He tossed the papers back onto the coffee table. "Shel, I hate to break this to you, but—"

"Yeah, I know. Tasha isn't real. But…God, this sounds insane…Jake, she talks to me. I can hear her like she's in the room with me, and I'm here all by myself, so I talk back to her."

Jake just sat there, and Shelby supposed it was because he was too flabbergasted to do anything else. He appeared to be thinking, so she remained quiet until he finally came up with something. "Okay then, what do you talk about?"

"Mostly I get bitchy with her because things are weird now and I blame her for it, and then she points out to me how everything that happened on the trip was basically my fault." Shelby stopped to poke around her noodles with her chopsticks, trying to piece together what she was trying to say. "I mean, it's not like we talk about the weather or plans for the weekend or anything else like that."

"Was it your fault?"

"I'm not sure. Maybe. I guess so."

Shelby Hutchinson, it's time for the truth.

"Okay, fine. You're right, it was my fault. It was me being all gee-whiz, look at the hot Russian babe with the great ass, and sure I'll go with you, and every other dumbshit thing I did. But you have to admit you set me up."

"I didn't set you up. Wait, you weren't talking to me, were you?"

"No, Jake, I wasn't. Sorry. Happens sometimes."

Jake stared back with a look Shelby couldn't quite decipher. "Have you called the guy from the vacation place again? What was his name?"

"Andrew. And yes, I talked to him just before you got here. He just gives me a lot of noise about how I'll be fine, and no one else has ever had any problems, so frankly, I don't ever want to talk to him again."

"I get that. So here's something I don't understand." Shelby waited patiently. "If Tasha, who is now living in your head, is the one who shot you, aren't you like, I don't know, scared shitless of her? I mean, every time you have a seizure, you wake up terrified, but now you're having conversations with her. I'm totally confused."

Shelby stared. She was confused as well but tried to piece together her thoughts. "Okay, I'm not sure. It's like I am scared of her, but it's kind of not really her. Jeez, that sounds stupid. Of course it's not really her, but it kind of is her." Jake stared as if he didn't understand, but how could he? Shelby didn't understand it herself, so she kept thinking out loud. "It's like this, Jake. When she talks to me in my head, she's the Tasha that helped me while I was on the trip. She taught me how to fight and made sure I was safe." Shelby rolled her eyes. "Yeah, well, safe except for that executing me part, but she took really good care of me for three days. Made sure I got fed and had a place to sleep, and other, well, you know, things and stuff." Shelby felt the blush rising up her neck while her thoughts drifted back to a particular vodka-fueled roll in the hay. "Never mind. Anyway, it's like she was a nice person who did one really shitty thing and so when I have a seizure and wake up, my head hurts and I can only think of that one bad thing, and I'm scared of that more than anything else that she did. Besides, I don't figure she can really hurt me because we're not in the Head Trip anymore."

"Are you sure about that?"

"I'm not sure about anything anymore. All I wanted to do was go on vacation, and now my life is seizures, headaches, and blackouts, and I have no idea what to do about it." Shelby shrugged and picked at her noodles.

"I get that too. So what's next? Are you going to tell the doctors about, you know, the heavily armed Russian badass with the great butt who is apparently living in your head?"

"Um, no...don't think so." She gave Jake a pleading glance. "This whole thing already makes me feel like I'm crazy. I certainly don't need a diagnosis of schizophrenia to make it official. Besides, you know how things are at the hospital. We all work together and it would only be a matter of time before people started to talk. Great. That's just what I need." She stopped to lean forward, offering Jake her own approximation of how the conversation would go. "Oh, hey, did you hear about Shelby Hutchinson, you know, the big geek who runs Information Systems? Apparently she has an imaginary Russian spy who lives in her head." Shelby lowered her voice to a whisper. "I hear they've even done it." She held up two fingers. "Twice." Shelby flopped back into the sofa. "I have no idea what to do about it."

"It sounds like a programming glitch," Jake said through a mouthful of noodles.

"Programming glitch?"

"Sure. Think about it. Head Trip and their whole fantasy vacation concept is nothing but a mega-tricked-out computer program, but instead of a computer, the program runs in your head. Mother Nature's own supercomputer, right?"

"Right, so if something interrupts the normal flow of the program, it gets buggy. And then you get a glitch. Jeez, Jake, why didn't I think of that? It's so simple. Now what?" She gave

Jake a questioning look, which he returned with one of his own. "I must have skipped Debugging the Human Brain 101 when I was an undergrad."

"Yeah, I missed that one too." He scratched his head. "While this may just be a theory, it seems to me you need to call your buddy Andrew again and shake him down a little."

"Yeah. Squirrelly little rodent. Telling me twice now that everything is fine and dandy." She crossed her arms over her chest with a resolute grunt and reached up to rub at the fading sore spot on her forehead. "Asshole."

"Yeah, well, I'm starting to think you're completely full of shit." Shelby snapped her phone closed. "I guess I'll just have to get to the bottom of this myself." Her third call to Andrew in as many days had proven fruitless. Once again, he was full of assurances that she'd be fine and everything would just clear up on its own. He had even offered to pay her medical bills this time. "I still think it's bullshit."

Before she could get even more pissed off, her phone chirped in her hand. It was Jake.

"So did you finally get a hold of him?"

"Yeah, I did. He's a weasel."

"You didn't find anything out?"

"Not a fucking thing. He's still trying to tell me it'll all just go away in a day or two." She headed to the kitchen for a fresh can of Coke. "I'm really sensing that something isn't right here. He sounds too much like a used car salesman."

"That's not good, Shel. How about if I come over after work and help you dig around a little online?"

"That's nice, Jake. Thank you."

Shelby stopped staring at her computer and rubbed her eyes, partly from fatigue, but mostly in frustration. All of her attempts to find out anything about Head Trip clients who had had a similar experience had come to dead ends. Maybe a fresh outlook was what she needed. Since Jake had offered to come by after work, she took a chance that since she was the head of the department, she could cajole him into leaving work early.

His phone rang twice before he picked up. "Hey, Shel. What's up?"

"Are you still coming over?"

"Actually—" Shelby's door buzzer went off. "I'm here." He smiled and waved at the front door video camera.

"Oh. Cool." She pressed the buzzer to let him in. "It's kind of early."

"Well, yeah, but I made some noise about bringing some work over here, so no one questioned that I left an hour early." Jake handed Shelby a small stack of data disks.

"What are these for?"

"I figured that since your buddy Andrew was being such a squirrelly little rat and not telling you anything, maybe he's got something to hide."

"Yeah, and what's on these?"

"Hacker codes."

"Hacker codes? I thought you didn't do this anymore. It's illegal." Shelby tried to act offended, but the more she thought about it, he was probably right.

"Don't get sanctimonious on me now. We need to find out if he's lying to you, and I can't think of any other way. Can you?"

"No, I can't, but we have to be careful."

"C'mon, Shel, it's me. I used to be good at this." He patted her shoulder, attempting to instill a little confidence. "Just like riding a bike." He gave Shelby a gentle shove toward her computer. "Pop one of those bad boys in there and let's see if we can find out what Head Trip is really all about."

❖

"I'm just not sure about this, Jake." Shelby pulled the collar of her ski jacket closer around her ears. The early evening was cold and she had once again left home without her hat.

"You had to get out of your apartment. It's been four days and, quite honestly, you needed to blow the stink off." Jake must have sensed Shelby's evil glower of disapproval, amending his statement to something a touch more gentle. "Not that you literally stunk, but—"

"Yeah, I get it." Shelby knew her self-imposed exile probably wasn't good for her, but she'd been so afraid to leave the house, Jake had finally pushed her toward the shower and dragged her bodily from her apartment. He was probably right. "It's just hard."

"And I get that. I'm right here," Jake wrapped a protective arm around her shoulders. "I'm not going to let anything bad happen." He squeezed the back of her neck. It felt nice, safe. "It's just Starbucks."

"I know." The headaches seemed a little better, and the frequency of seizures seemed to have slowed down, so maybe nothing would happen. She hoped so anyway. "Not like I'm going to run into any heavily armed Russian agents. Well, despite the one who talks to me at home."

"Nope, no bad guys. It'll be fine." He pulled the door to the coffee shop open and ushered Shelby through.

She stopped in the doorway just long enough to warm up and take a long sniff. "Ah, yes, coffee fixes everything."

"My treat. Have at it."

"Thanks, buddy." Shelby leaned on the counter with both hands and placed her order. "Peppermint mocha, please."

The barista smiled back. "Whipped cream?"

"Oh, yeah, hook me up." Shelby stood to one side while Jake ordered a caramel macchiato for himself and dug his wallet out of his coat to pay for their order. Shelby got distracted by the display of coffee mugs for sale. She stopped when she spotted something in the corner of the shop that filled her with an eerie kind of dread. A woman, sitting alone at a table, writing furiously in a notebook. A chocolate-brown ponytail spilled down the back of her black sweater. "Oh, shit," Shelby said quietly into the palm of her hand, which had somehow found its way up to cover her mouth.

"Shel, what's wrong? You look like you've seen a ghost."

"What?"

"Are you in pain? What's up?"

"Over there, in the corner." She pointed toward the woman. "I just thought I recognized her."

"Who, the gal with the notebook?"

"Yeah, I just thought...Never mind, it's crazy." Shelby needed to believe that. And she did, until the mystery woman in the corner turned around. There were the crystal blue eyes. Shelby gasped when she saw them, and she began to feel a little sick as she registered the rest of the woman's face. Same eyes, same angular jaw, same crooked grin. It was Tasha.

"Oh, shit again. Jake, get me out of here."

"But, what about..." He motioned toward the counter and their unfinished coffee order.

"Now." Shelby grabbed the sleeve of Jake's coat. "Have to leave, have to get out."

Shelby felt a stab of pain in her head. "Not again." She kept pulling at Jake's coat, but now it was to keep from falling when the headache escalated and she realized what was about to happen. "Jake, help—"

She never finished her sentence before darkness closed in again.

❖

"Oh, shit. She shot me!" Shelby's hand flew up to a spot on her forehead. She could feel the wound, red hot, surely bleeding freely. But her hand came away clean and dry. "What the fuck?"

"Shelby. Shelby Hutchinson. Wake up."

A male voice. Shelby was disoriented. "What?" she asked through the fog of searing pain and confusion. "What happened?" She tried to sit up, but strong arms pinned her shoulders to the ground, keeping her immobile. "Where am I?" She felt around on the floor, trying to ground herself, figure out what happened. Her hands slid on something unidentifiable.

"Shel, sweetie, lie still. You're okay now."

Things were crawling back into focus. Shelby took a long breath and attempted to collect her wits. Not easy considering she still wasn't sure why she was on the ground, rubbing at an imaginary gunshot wound. "Oh, wait a minute…" It was coming back. "Jake?"

"Yeah, Shel, it's me, Jake. Take it easy."

"I'm fine, all kinds of fine here."

"Bullshit."

Things continued to come into focus. Jake, his smile extending all the way to his dark brown eyes, loomed over her. Shelby relaxed a little and took a long breath to try to quell the deep ache in her head. "Ow." Her head really hurt. "Jake, can you get me some—"

"Here you go."

"Thanks." Jake turned around and accepted a cup of ice from someone Shelby didn't recognize. Wait a minute. She did recognize her.

"Oh, shit. Tasha." Shelby scrabbled with her hands on the floor, trying but failing to move anywhere. She had to get away.

But she wasn't going anywhere. Apparently, Shelby had managed to pull the music display over when she went down. Her hands slid on the spilled disks, serving to escalate her panic. "Help me…don't let her—"

Jake grabbed her arms, pinning her to the floor, but Shelby

was having none of it. "Calm down. No one did anything to you." She continued to struggle in an attempt to escape, but he was just too big. Shelby wasn't going anywhere. "You had another seizure."

"Jake, please." She was desperate for him to understand how scared she was. "It's her. Don't let her near—"

Jake took her by the chin and urged her to look at him. "Who do you see? What's wrong?"

She tried to focus through the pain and the frightening memory of the gun going off in her face. It wasn't easy, especially considering she was now looking at the face of the woman who had pulled the trigger. Shelby wiggled her shoulders, freeing herself from Jake's grasp. "Tasha." She held a shaking hand up and pointed toward the woman. "She's Tasha."

"What Tasha? The Russian spy?" He lowered his voice to whisper. "The one who talks—"

"Yes. That Russian spy." She closed her eyes in the hope it would drive the image of Tasha from her vision. When she opened them, Tasha was still there. Shelby started to cry. "Please, please, don't let her hurt me."

"What is she talking about?" Tasha's look-alike appeared to be as confused as Jake did. "I didn't do anything." Weird. Not a trace of Tasha's Russian accent.

Jake turned to answer. "I know you didn't. She'll be okay."

To make things worse, the manager of the Starbucks appeared behind Jake. "Is everything okay over here? Do I need to call an ambulance?"

"No." Shelby began to panic again. She didn't want to go back to the hospital. "No ambulance. I'll be okay." She didn't necessarily believe it, but all she wanted was to go home.

Jake took care of it. "No, she'll be fine in a few minutes." The manager silently acknowledged Jake's answer and went back to wherever he had come from.

Something appeared in her peripheral vision. Shelby was such a mess at this point she tried to duck and hide.

"Shel. Please, take it easy. It's just ice." Jake pointed toward the cup in his right hand. "And this kind person…" He motioned toward the Tasha clone. "What's your name?"

"Trish."

Jake took a long breath. "Trish here saw you were having trouble and she got you a cup of ice."

Head almost clear, Shelby took in every detail. Same chocolate brown hair, crystal blue eyes, everything identical. She sure looked like Tasha. Shelby still couldn't quite believe what she was seeing. She shrugged and gave a weak smile to Tasha's doppelganger, who looked more than a little puzzled.

"What did you mean by Russian spy?" The woman offered up her own version of the dumbfounded expression. "I'm not a spy." She looked over to Jake for support. "Is she okay? I mean, did she hit her head or something?"

Jake didn't answer. He just stared at the woman and cocked his head. "She sure looks like the picture." He turned back toward Shelby. "Doesn't she?"

"It's uncanny." Shelby still wasn't sure how she felt. Maybe not quite terrified anymore, but definitely curious with a healthy dose of apprehension. "And you're certain you're not a Russian spy sent here through a rift in time from 1985 just to fuck with me some more?" Shelby winced, but it had to be said. She sat up, rubbed at her forehead, and accepted the cup of ice from Jake.

"What?" Trish looked to Jake again. "Are you sure she didn't hit her head?"

"No, I didn't hit my head. I had a seizure because someone who looks exactly like you shot me in the head." Shelby held the ice to the sore spot on her face and held up her free hand to Jake for assistance up from the floor. He obliged and held on until Shelby felt stable enough to let go. "No kidding. Fine and dandy here."

"Shot you in the head? What on earth are you talking about? Someone shot you in the head?"

"Yes, well, sort of, not really, but it's a long story." Boy, was that an understatement.

"I can assure you—"

"Shelby Hutchinson," Jake said.

"I can assure you, Shelby Hutchinson, I am nothing but a simple writer for *Chicago Weekly E-zine*. I don't know anything about Russian spies, and I certainly have no intention of, as you so eloquently put it, fucking with you."

Shelby cringed again, partly because of the way Trish had said her name, and partly because she had apparently offended Trish with her language. "Sorry about that."

"Apology accepted," Trish answered with a single nod.

"But you look exactly like her." Shelby still couldn't get over the resemblance. There had to be a connection. It was too bizarre.

"Exactly like whom?" Trish offered a timid smile. "I've got a table in the corner. You could tell me your long story. And your boyfriend too. Unless you need to go, what with the seizure and all."

"No...I mean yes, thank you. And he's not my boyfriend, despite being a boy and my friend." She rolled her eyes. "Sitting down is probably a good idea." Shelby still felt a little like she was listing on the deck of a boat in a storm. "Haven't quite got my sea legs yet." Jake held her arm to steady her as Shelby wobbled a little.

"Whoa there, kiddo. I've got you."

"Thanks." Shelby turned to look at Trish, but found she still couldn't make eye contact. It was just too weird. "This is Jake, by the way."

"Nice to meet you." Jake extended a hand toward Trish, who shook it as she introduced herself in return.

"Patricia Aronoff. My friends call me Trish."

Shelby studied Trish's face, noting there was something there that Tasha didn't have. There was a warmth to her smile that Shelby found comforting. Jake helped Shelby to a chair, got her situated, and scurried off to get their drinks from the counter. She still couldn't look Trish in the eye.

"Are you sure you're okay? You, um, went down pretty hard," Trish said.

"No, I'm okay. It happens once in a while. Don't worry about it."

"But you said something about me shooting you in the head, whatever that means. What were you talking about?"

Shelby adjusted the cup of ice on her forehead. "It's like this: I took a virtual vacation, things didn't work out right, and you shot me in the head. Well, we've established that in reality it wasn't you, but damn, you could be her twin." Shelby finally braved a closer look. She found another difference. Trish's eyes were the same clear blue, but they weren't cold like Tasha's. "Your eyes are a little different." They were warm and inviting, and Shelby thought, trustworthy. Oh, shit. Not again.

"A virtual vacation?"

"Have you heard of it? They implant memories of fantasy vacations."

Trish furrowed her brow. "Do you mean Head Trip?"

Shelby was a little surprised. "Yeah, Head Trip. That's the place. Have you been there, taken a vacation?"

"Early last week." Trish leafed through her notebook until she found what she had been looking for. "Tuesday afternoon, for a piece I'm working on. I talked to a guy, a technician with blond hair—"

"Andrew?" Shelby said.

"Yes, Andrew. Squirrelly sort of guy."

"Yeah, that's him." Shelby sneered. "Rodent."

"You know, he struck me that way too. I was researching the virtual vacation phenomenon, so I went as far as to do their mapping procedure, but the whole thing kind of freaked me out. Since I had enough information for my article, I decided to forgo the vacation."

Shelby set down her cup of ice and rubbed idly at her forehead. "I should have skipped it too."

"Why? What happened?"

Shelby wasn't exactly sure what motivated her to want to tell Trish the whole sordid tale, but she did. "Are you sure you want to hear this?"

"Yes, I do, unless you don't feel up to it."

"Feel up to what?" Jake asked as he returned with Shelby's coffee.

"Trish wants to know all about Head Trip." Trish found a clean page in her notebook. Shelby tentatively began to tell the tale of her Head Trip vacation, the shooting, and the rude awakening when it was over. "It's been several days now, and I'm very obviously still having some problems."

"I noticed that." Trish offered a timid grin. "The thing I'm still unclear about is how the character in your vacation looked like me. I did the mapping but I never agreed to allow them to use me in anyone else's trip." She got a funny look on her face. "Exactly how much of me did they use?"

Shelby felt the blush begin to creep its way up her neck.

It's again time for truth, Shelby Hutchinson.

Shelby gritted her teeth and answered under her breath, "Yeah, I know." She struggled to explain. "Um, pretty much, you know…" The blush kept rising. "Everything."

"Everything?" Shelby saw the metaphorical light bulb when it flashed on over Trish's head. "Everything, as in—"

"Yep, everything." Shelby stared into her coffee.

"I'm not sure I believe you." Trish scratched her head. "They wouldn't actually—"

Shelby lobbed a grenade. "You have a freckle on your right shoulder blade," she said and pointed toward her right hip, "and a scar, here, from I don't know what. I just assumed it was probably from a knife fight."

"Knife fight? What? No. Appendectomy." Trish's mouth hung open. "About ten years ago. And yes, freckle, right shoulder blade." Her expression changed to one of horror. "How do you know this? Oh God, what did we do?"

"Again, I say everything. You know?" The blush became so hot that Shelby feared her ears might catch fire. She wanted to crawl under the table. Trish looked like she did as well.

"Really?" Just for a second, Shelby would have sworn Trish wasn't totally offended by the idea. But then it was gone again. "Oh my God."

"The second time, we were both drunk, so maybe that helps." Shelby rolled her eyes. Trish still looked horrified. "Or not."

Trish was ignoring her notebook. "The second time? Drunk?" She looked like she wanted to throw up. "I don't even drink." She also looked like she wanted to cry. "I feel so violated."

"I'm right there with you." Shelby picked up her cup of ice and reapplied it to her forehead. "Not exactly feeling the love over this way either."

"I'm so sorry, but—" Trish stopped, apparently too flabbergasted to speak.

Shelby was out of things to say as well. Jake broke the silence.

"You're a reporter or something like that, right?" He pointed to her notebook. "Can you do something? Tell someone?"

Trish didn't exactly look comfortable with the idea. "I'm not sure. I mean, I could talk to my editor."

For the first time since she got back from her vacation, Shelby felt a glimmer of hope. "Maybe if...think about this. What if something is going on there? You know, Andrew and his vermin vibe...we both saw it." Trish nodded. "Every time I call him he says I'll be fine. Other people were fine...blah, blah, blah...Well, anyway, maybe someone needs to talk to these 'other people' and find out if they are fine and dandy."

Jake jumped in and pointed at Trish. "And you're the one researching the whole virtual vacation thing. Evil corporate bastards."

Trish rubbed her chin. "Sounds interesting, but how do you propose we get those names? I'm sure Rat Boy isn't going to be overly forthcoming with that kind of information. Know any hackers?"

"Shel could do it." Jake smiled as if it was the best idea he'd ever had. "She's a whiz."

"No," Shelby said. "I'm the director of Information Systems, not a random kid hacking into the Pentagon from his mom's basement." She stared back at Jake. "Besides, you're the reformed hacker, not me."

"What's the difference?" Jake asked. "She's really a whiz," he said to Trish.

Trish looked to Shelby, a hopeful expression on her face. "It would make my job immensely easier, and it helps you at the same time. I seriously want to know what's going on with these people."

It's time to face your fear, Shelby Hutchinson.

"Yes, you're right." She wasn't certain whether she was answering Trish or Tasha, but the answer was the same either way. Shelby resolutely stuck out her chin. "I'm sure I could manage something." She winced and returned the cup of ice to her forehead. "But it might have to wait until tomorrow."

"Sure, I understand. Are you sure you're all right?" Trish's hand came to rest comfortingly on Shelby's arm.

"Yeah, the headache is backing off, but I'm kind of wiped out."

Trish stuffed her notebook into her bag and stood. "Jake, you should take her home. Make sure she gets some rest. Here's my card. I'm going to do a little digging to see what I can come up with. We should talk later when you are a little more yourself. Can I get your number?"

"Sure." Shelby scribbled her number on a napkin and handed it to Trish.

"I'll be in touch. We'll get to the bottom of this."

Shelby watched Trish walk out of Starbucks and wondered what the hell would happen next.

She is a take-charge woman, Shelby Hutchinson. You like that, no?

"Shut up, Tasha," she mumbled under her breath.

"I think Trish was right," said Jake. "Let's get you home."

Home sounded like a great idea. The comfort of her own four walls and no one trying to mess with her head. Well, no one but the imaginary Russian spy who lived there too, but who's counting? Shelby hauled herself out of her chair, relieved that the world wasn't spinning around her, and made her way to the door, well aware she was not the picture of poise and confidence Trish had been, but then Trish hadn't been floundering on the floor in the midst of a corporate-sponsored seizure either.

Shelby stepped out into the frigid night and pulled her jacket close against the chill.

"I'll go get the car, Shel. Will you be okay?"

"I'm fine, Jake. Go get the car."

❖

The insistent buzz of her cell phone woke Shelby from a foggy dream. She reached for her phone, spilling the glass of water on her bedside table.

"Shit. Hello?"

"Good morning to you too. This is Trish. I have news."

Trish. Head Trip. Tasha? No, Trish. Shelby sat up, pulling the covers with her.

"Hi, Trish. I'm sorry. I spilled my water. What time is it?"

"It's ten thirty. Sorry if I woke you, but we have an appointment."

"We do?"

"Yep, with one Andrew the Rat Boy at one."

The fog was beginning to clear, and replacing it was a

combination of apprehension and anticipation. "We're going to Head Trip together?"

"After we met yesterday, I went back to the office and did some digging around. I have a couple contacts here and there at hospitals in the city. It seems you are definitely not the only Head Trip customer to have had health problems after their vacation. I don't have names, but I do have numbers and symptoms. I called Andrew and told him we were coming to see him so he'd better clear his calendar."

Take-charge woman, indeed! "Wow, okay, I'll meet you there at one. Trish? What is it we're going to say to him exactly?"

"Don't worry about it. Just follow my lead. I've got the power of the press behind me, and I'm going to use it. See you at one."

Shelby clicked her phone off and tossed it on the bed.

You need to be careful. She leads you into trouble, Shelby Hutchinson.

"You would know all about that, wouldn't you, Tasha?" She threw off her covers and went to the closet. "What does one wear to skewer a rat?"

Leather is always appropriate.

Shelby ran her hand down the buttery soft sleeve of her leather jacket. "You know, Tasha, on that I think we agree."

At 12:55, heart pounding, Shelby stood in front of the Head Trip offices waiting for Trish. A cab pulled up to the curb in front of her, and when the door opened, the first thing Shelby saw was a pair of long legs and fabulous shoes stepping onto the sidewalk. She knew she was staring, but they were truly great legs, followed by an impressive suit, topped off by a face she knew well, or at least thought she did. By the time Trish had gracefully unfurled from the cab, Shelby had completely forgotten why she was

there. This woman was not Tasha, the spy; neither was she Trish, the concerned bystander. She was Patricia Aronoff, force to be reckoned with.

"Hey, Shelby." Trish straightened the jacket of her navy blue pinstripe suit. "Are you ready to do this?"

For the first time in a long time, Shelby felt ready for nearly anything. "Let's go."

The bravado lasted until they were ushered into Andrew's office by his assistant. He sat behind his desk, staring at a computer screen and typing furiously.

"Have a seat, ladies. I will be with you in just a moment."

Shelby sat in one of the two standard-issue office chairs in front of Andrew's desk. She felt like she had been called to the principal's office, but as she remembered it, her principal's desk had always been cluttered with papers and files and pictures of his family. Andrew's desk was completely clear, except for his computer. It was a little frightening, this monument to ruthless efficiency.

She glanced over at Trish, whose face had set into a stony mask. She squared her shoulders and sat up a little straighter.

Andrew closed the file he was working on and turned toward Shelby and Trish. "Now, what can I do for you both? I must say I was a bit surprised by your phone call, Miss Aronoff, and your insistence on meeting."

"And yet, you took the meeting, didn't you, Andrew? It has come to my attention that you have evidently used my image without my permission in someone else's Head Trip vacation. This is a completely unacceptable situation."

Andrew leaned back in his chair, a vision of smug assurance. "Miss Aronoff, I'm sure you are mistaken. We do not use client profiles in other clients' vacations unless specifically requested by both parties. For instance, a couple who wish to vacation together, but never without written permission."

"Then how is it that Trish ended up in my vacation?" Shelby wanted to smack that smarmy look right off his face.

Andrew leaned forward, suddenly the picture of concern. "Miss Hutchinson, I wondered about your presence here. I think this all begins to make a little more sense. I'm sure your doctors have explained to you that the seizures you have recently experienced can affect your memories. I seem to remember a character from your vacation who had a passing resemblance to Miss Aronoff—same hair color, perhaps eye color, but I can assure you—"

"Assure me of what? That it wasn't Trish in my vacation? That she didn't blow my brains out? That the seizures are a minor setback? That Tasha isn't still in my head?" Oops. That might have been a little too much. Her heart was pounding and she could feel the pinprick beginnings of a headache forming on a spot just over her left eye. The only thing keeping her from coming out of the chair and leaping across Andrew's desk was Trish's hand on her arm.

"What about that, Andrew?" asked Trish. "What about her seizures?"

"Since the two of you are obviously well acquainted, I'm sure Miss Hutchinson has told you we have agreed to cover her medical bills and only have her best interests at heart."

"Is that what you told the others as well?"

Andrew stared unblinking at Trish for a moment. Every trace of solicitousness was gone now. "What others?" he asked through tight lips.

Trish reached into her bag and withdrew a notebook. She flipped through a few pages. "Patient A, Northwest Memorial, returned from vacation complaining of migraines. Patient B, also Northwest Memorial, presented with seizures and some memory loss upon returning from vacation. Patient C, St. Stephens Hospital, presented with seizures, followed by loss of vision. Interestingly, all after taking a Head Trip vacation. There are more here, Andrew, but I'm sure you know that. I'm tired of playing games. You used my profile without permission, which is most definitely a breach of ethics and a violation of my privacy. Add to that the fact there are people who are being injured by your technology. What kind of business are you running here?"

"A very profitable one, Miss Aronoff, as I am sure you know. That's what this is all about, isn't it? You two are in cahoots trying to extort money from this company." He turned to Shelby. "Where did you find her, Miss Hutchinson? Or have you known each other all along? Was this a setup from the beginning? We have offered, very generously I might add, to pay your medical expenses as a sign of good faith, but that is all you will receive from us. And as for you, Miss Aronoff, the very idea we would use your likeness in another vacation scenario is ridiculous. We pay individuals for the use of their profiles. If there was a similarity between you and the woman in Miss Hutchinson's scenario, it was because she requested someone of your type. Though for the life of me I can't imagine why. Of course, if you two have been in on this all along then you know that, don't you? I have had quite enough of this. Please leave."

Andrew gestured toward the door, and Shelby sat in stunned silence at his ridiculous rant.

Trish rose from her chair and smoothed her skirt. "You will be hearing from my attorney."

Shelby followed Trish out of the office and to the elevator. "What the hell was that?" she asked when the doors to the elevator had closed.

"Wait." Trish pointed to the security cameras.

They rode the elevator in silence, thoughts tumbling around in Shelby's head. She hadn't imagined Andrew's threatening tone, and frankly, it scared her. They reached street level and stepped out into the bitter Chicago wind. "So now what? That was a bust."

"Are you kidding? We learned a lot. One, Andrew is a lying sack of shit. Did you see the way he never quite made eye contact? And the way he kept twisting the ring on his hand. I've interviewed a lot of people. I can spot a liar. Two, rather than being concerned about how I ended up in your vacation scenario, he 'knew' I couldn't have. The customer is always right. He should have been bending over backward to try to come up with an answer. Instead, he went on the offensive a little too quickly, if you ask me. Makes me wonder if he hasn't given a similar speech before, you know?"

"Yeah, he did turn it around awful quick, but if he's given that speech before, then this is a little scary. How many people were on your hospital list?"

"Eight, from three hospitals. I don't have a lot of details, and I had to call in favors to get what I got, but there is definitely something here. Look, I need to get back to the office. I wish I could change first." Trish stepped off the curb to hail a cab.

"You mean that's not what you usually wear to work?"

Trish laughed as a Yellow Cab pulled up. "God, no. Everyone at the office will think I've been to a funeral. I'll call you."

The car door slammed and the taxi pulled away. Shelby stepped back into the crush of passersby and right into someone's path. The other person bumped Shelby hard and muttered, "Excuse me," through a heavy woolen scarf. Shelby was about to respond when she felt something being pushed into her hand. Instinctively, she took the small piece of paper and crumpled it into her pocket, then thought better of it.

"Hey, wait a minute!" Shelby turned, but all she could see was a crowd of hunched shoulders and knitwear. She pulled off a mitten and fished the paper out of her pocket. It was a large fuchsia sticky note with three lines scribbled on it:

I have information for you about your vacation.
Meet me at O'Donnell's Pub
9:00 tonight

Ah, Shelby Hutchinson, the plot is thickening, yes?
"It looks like it, Tasha. It absolutely does."

CHAPTER ELEVEN

Shel, you are not going off to meet some stranger at a bar in the middle of the night by yourself!"

Shelby poured herself another cup of coffee while Jake stomped around her kitchen. "Nine o'clock is hardly the middle of the night. O'Donnell's is a very respectable pub. I'll be fine."

"Do you even know if it was a man or a woman who gave you this note?"

"I think it was a woman."

"You think?"

"Well, yeah, I looked her right in the eye over the scarf she was wearing. She had to be about my height—kind of short for a man. And the scarf was purple. I don't know too many guys who would wear that shade of purple. Besides, what difference does it make? It's not like I'm going anywhere with this person. I'll just get the information and then come home. You can wait for me. It'll be okay."

"Famous last words."

Shelby set her cup on the table. "Cut it out. You are being a Nelly. I know the note is cloak and dagger, but let's not get carried away. It's not like this woman is a Russian spy who's going to blow my brains out."

It's not funny, Shelby Hutchinson.

"That's not funny, Shel."

"Yes, it is, both of you!" Shelby caught Jake's puzzled glance and shook her head. "Never mind. Don't you get it? The cloak-and-dagger spy stuff was just a fantasy. That's not real life, but these seizures sure as hell are real. If you had seen that damned Andrew sitting there looking all smug, acting like the whole situation is a figment of my imagination. I'll tell you one thing, if it's all in my head it's because he put it there. If I have a chance to get this guy, I have to take it."

Jake sighed. "I understand, but please be careful. I'm going to wait here until you get back."

"Yes, Mom." Shelby hugged him. "I'll be fine."

❖

At precisely nine o'clock, Shelby's cab pulled into a parking spot on McClaren about halfway down the block from O'Donnell's. Her stomach was doing flip-flops, and she was finding it hard to open the door. Regardless of how confident she had sounded in her kitchen, this meeting was freaking her out. She took a deep breath, shoved some money at the cabbie, and opened her car door. The wind blasted through the car and took her fear with it. She would rather face whatever was coming while in the toasty confines of a bar rather than sit out here and freeze to death in a cab that smelled vaguely of fish.

O'Donnell's was like a lot of pubs: dark wood, scarred tables, loud voices. The bar itself sat opposite the front door. It ran almost the length of the pub. Three bartenders stood behind it pouring beer and mixing drinks with speed and evidently a good bit of accuracy. Shelby watched as a tall mug sailed down the bar into its owner's waiting hands.

She slipped onto a bar stool and stuffed her mittens into the pocket of her leather jacket. Before she had a chance to size up her neighbors at the bar, one of the bartenders appeared in front of her, placing a napkin on the bar.

"What'll you have?"

She ordered a Killian's figuring she couldn't go wrong with that in an Irish pub, though she had noticed the bartender had no sign of a brogue. She was a little disappointed at that. She had a thing for accents. The bartender brought her beer, and she left a ten on the bar. Shelby studied the bar's patrons. None of them looked anything like the person she had run into on the street outside of the Head Trip offices. But that was because no one in here was still wearing a scarf. She would have to wait. Maybe it was all just a joke and this was a complete waste of time. She sipped her beer and stared at the mirror over the bar back.

Lost in thought, she almost didn't notice when someone took the bar stool next to hers. The bartender came to take the new order and had returned with a drink before Shelby bothered to glance in the newcomer's direction. She was a lovely girl, mid twenties, short red hair, and something about the eyes...

"Yes, Miss Hutchinson, it's me. Could you please stop staring? You'll attract attention and neither one of us needs that."

"I'm sorry. You look familiar. I mean, not from this afternoon. I could barely see you on the street. Why do I know you?"

"My name is Lois Evans. I was one of the technicians at Head Trip who oversaw your vacation."

Shelby had a sudden flash of memory of Lois in the room as she was being prepared for her vacation. "I think I remember, but you'll understand things from that whole experience are kind of fuzzy." Shelby found it hard to keep the anger from her voice.

"I do understand, believe me." Lois sipped her drink, which looked to Shelby to be about three fingers of scotch. "I heard you came in to the office today and met with Andrew."

"Yes, I did, for all the good it did."

"It did something. After you left, Andrew went on a rampage. He shut the system down 'for maintenance' he said, but I don't believe that for a minute. What did you say to him?"

Warning sirens went off in Shelby's head. "Um, Lois, you asked me to meet you to give me information, not get info from me. Did Andrew send you?"

Lois sat up straighter. "God no. He would kill me if he knew I was here. It takes a lot to fluster Andrew. I figured whatever you said had to be big. Anyway, I guess I got tired of waiting for Andrew to do something about all of this. He told me he would, and after the problems with your scenario, I thought he was finally coming around. But he keeps putting me off, and I think it's because there is something seriously flawed in the technology. I'm afraid somebody is going to get killed."

"Okay, Lois. Slow down. Tell me what's going on at Head Trip."

Lois took another sip of her drink before launching into her story. "I started working at Head Trip right out of college. In the beginning, we were all practically giddy because what we were doing was so new and cutting edge. There were occasional problems, just little things. Someone didn't like the way their vacation turned out or whatever. We figured that was due to not having enough information on our clients. The interview process and mapping process became more extensive. Andrew hired more programmers to deal with the complexity of the programming. At about the same time, he started courting government agencies, looking for contracts from the defense department and the like. I didn't know about it. I don't think most of us did. Andrew was pushing us hard to upgrade the system and the quality of the virtual experience. He wanted it as lifelike as possible, as keyed in to the client's wishes as we could possibly make it."

"Well, you certainly succeeded. It was very realistic, maybe too realistic for me."

"You weren't the only one."

"Tell me." Shelby signaled the bartender for two more drinks.

"Andrew started having meetings in the office with official-looking guys in dark suits. That's not the kind of people we usually see at Head Trip. He wanted us to launch the improvements before we had completed testing. He wanted the suits to see the technology in action. We were all pretty nervous because Andrew was pushing so hard, but we were confident in the programming and we went ahead. The test runs went well, and we began to use the new programming for our everyday clients. A few weeks later, money started rolling in. Andrew remodeled the office, said we needed to present a certain image to attract important clientele. He was suddenly driving a new car, and he didn't keep it to himself either. We all got raises to compensate for all the overtime we had been putting in, and Head Trip was the happiest place on earth. Until the first accident."

"What happened?" asked Shelby.

"It was a hiccup in the system. The client was on a vacation, rock climbing in Yosemite. This guy was an expert climber. He even consulted with us before he took his trip to help perfect the scenario. He fell while he was climbing, and I guess he died in the scenario because he woke abruptly. No one was in the room until the alarms went off, but we were in there within seconds. We calmed him down, gave him a credit, and suggested he go get checked out at the hospital. Really, we didn't think much of it. Shit happens with computers. There is always the potential for error, but we thought we were well within acceptable parameters. Now, I just don't know."

"What happened to him, to the climber?"

Lois took a long slug of her drink. "He's in a coma. He started having bad headaches. He said he felt like his skull was being crushed."

Shelby idly rubbed at her forehead. "Like he fell off a cliff and landed on his head."

"Right," Lois said. "Anyway, one night he had a major seizure and slipped into a coma. When he didn't show up to work, his boss called the police, and they broke into his apartment. Head Trip is paying for a very expensive clinic stay in another state."

"How do you know this?"

"Because I've been there since the beginning. I have clearance, access to everything. At least I did until today. When Andrew shut down the system, he also canceled everyone's clearance. He says we'll be up and running again next week, and we'll all be paid for the time off. That's when I knew something was up. Andrew isn't that generous."

"So what about my vacation? What happened?"

"I can only assume you died in your scenario."

Shelby rubbed at her forehead and nodded. "Getting shot in the head will do that, yeah, but that wasn't part of what I asked for on my vacation. I mean I wanted a spy adventure, sure, but I was supposed to be the hero, not the dipshit who gets shot in the head for being so stupid."

"I know. That climber didn't pay to fall off the mountain either. You see, the programming has a certain amount of free will. It generates responses to the client's actions according to the information it collects from the mapping procedure. We always knew there was potential for a vacation to end unsatisfactorily. You know, geeky guy can't actually get the supermodel into bed, that sort of thing, but we didn't imagine any of this would happen. We had no way of anticipating that any of this could have physical ramifications outside of the virtual scenario."

"So what do you think happened in my trip? Why am I having seizures and why is Tasha still talking to me?"

Lois looked surprised. "Tasha is still talking to you? Wasn't she the bad guy in your scenario?"

Shelby nodded and sipped at her drink. "Yeah, that's exactly what she was. She was also based on a physical scan of a real person who never gave her permission for Andrew to use her image."

Lois rolled her eyes. "Andrew has been doing that. Flip-flopping scanned images from other people without their knowledge so he doesn't have to pay for the rights."

"Asshole. That certainly explains how Trish wound up in my vacation."

"It does. And I'm pretty sure that's why Tasha is still talking to you. It's hard to explain." Lois swirled her scotch and took another long drink.

"Try. I'm a programmer too. Explain it to me."

"Okay. It's like this. When we program characters for each vacation, we build a complete individual. The personality, physical characteristics, everything. So since your Tasha was a hybrid program, when you died in the scenario, the program crashed. That's why you got thrown out of the trip and it also explains why she's still in your head. It's kind of like, what was the name of that really buggy old word processing program that everyone used to use?"

"Microsoft Office?"

"Yeah, that one. I learned about it in school. It used to do this thing. If your computer shut down unexpectedly while you were working on a document, Office would get wonky. Sometimes your work would disappear, sometimes it would add really bizarre characters and numbers, stuff like that." Lois took another drink. "You never knew what would happen, so most people just got used to hitting the Save button a lot. Crappy old program."

"It really was. But I'm still not sure that I understand how that applies to my Head Trip."

Lois blew out a long breath and scratched at her head. "The way the vacation works is that we write a computer program and the new technology allows us to use your brain like a hard drive. When your scenario crashed, the Tasha program continued to run in your brain. It's basically implanted memories, except—"

"Except, now instead of running on your mega system, it's—"

"Running in your head. Right. And the only way to get it to stop is to go back into your scenario and let it play out. Shut the program down properly. That should also shut down the program in your head, and hopefully, stop your headaches and seizures."

"Should? Hopefully?" Shelby didn't like the idea of going back into her Head Trip and dealing with Tasha face-to-face. "I don't want to go back in there. Are you certain?"

"Yes." Lois was adamant. "I know that's what you need to do."

Shelby really didn't like that idea, but if it was necessary… "All right." She took a long swig of her drink. "Is this what the climber guy needs to do too? I mean, he's comatose in a hospital now, but—"

Lois shook her head. "We could do that, but he needs to be conscious for us to get access. I'm afraid he's had too much brain damage at this point."

"Makes sense." Shelby felt a little sick. She really had to go back and face Tasha one more time. "But once you knew people were suffering, why didn't it stop?"

"Money. Nothing else. Andrew decided he didn't want to pay outsiders for their mapping rights anymore. He began reusing client maps in other scenarios. I guess he figured no one would ever catch on, and he could always weasel his way out of it if anyone became suspicious."

"But what about the people who got hurt? The people like me?"

"At first, Andrew assured everyone he had hired outside contractors to help with the programming, to try to make the security protocols failsafe. I don't know if any of that was true. The only thing I know for sure is those guys in the suits turned out to be government types from the Department of Defense. Head Trip now has a huge contract with the U.S. government, which is extremely interested in using our technology for military simulations. I guess Andrew has decided there is no way he can give up the contract."

"We've got to tell someone, Lois. What's going to happen

when soldiers start lapsing into comas after they die in virtual training? This is crazy. There is no way we can let this happen."

"I know. That's why I came to you. When you showed up at the office today with Miss Aronoff, well, I told you how upset it made Andrew. I heard there was talk of an attorney, and I figured if you told the attorney what I have told you, then Andrew could be stopped."

"Why haven't you gone to the police?"

"Look, Miss Hutchinson, I could give you a whole lot of reasons, like all the problems fell within statistical norms, or every Head Trip client signs a release, and all of those reasons would be technically true. The thing is the situation is wrong. I know that at a gut level, and the only reason I haven't gone to the police is that I'm scared. Andrew flat-out scares me."

Shelby was afraid she was losing Lois. Maybe she shouldn't have bought that last drink for her. She leaned in close to Lois, who had put her head down on her folded arms. "Lois, I'm going to put you in a cab and send you home. Thank you for all your help. I'll let you know what I find out."

"Thank you, Miss Hutchinson. I'm sorry about all this. This should never have happened to you or anyone else. I'm fine, really. I can get home on my own."

"Not in your car." Shelby signaled to Mike. "Can I get a cab for me and one for my friend, please?"

Mike nodded and reached for the phone.

❖

Shelby burst through the door of her apartment, pulling off her mittens and unwrapping her scarf. "You will not believe what I just found out!"

She remembered that Jake had said he would wait for her, but pulled up when she saw who else was waiting for her in her kitchen. "Tash—Trish? What's going on?"

"Trish's apartment was broken into tonight, Shel."

She looked from Jake to Trish, taking in his worried expression and her exhaustion. She slipped onto the kitchen stool next to Trish and squeezed her arm. "What happened? Are you okay? Did you call the police?"

Trish took a sip from her wineglass and made a weak attempt at a smile. "I'm okay, and yes, I called the police. After I left you today, I went back to the office, and after I explained that I hadn't been to a funeral or a wedding or a job interview, I tried to find some info on Head Trip. I guess time got away from me, because when I looked up it was already six o'clock. I think it's probably a good thing I was late or I may have run into my visitors before they were done trashing my place. I didn't know anything until I walked into the apartment. The bastards had even locked the door on the way out. They completely wrecked the place, which pisses me off because they got what they wanted. They didn't need to cut up my mattress."

"What did they want?"

"The only thing missing from the apartment is my Head Trip contract."

"Well, we've got them then. What did the police say?"

"I didn't tell them. They thought it was probably meth addicts who broke in looking for money and then trashed the place when they didn't find any."

"I don't get it. Why didn't you tell them?"

Jake chimed in. "She didn't tell them because she got scared, Shel, and you should be too. These people aren't messing around, and they evidently know how to cover their tracks, not to mention send a message. Trish wanted to talk to you before she did anything else."

Shelby began to wonder how long these two had been sitting here plotting. "I'm sorry. I didn't mean to push. It's just that I found out some stuff about Head Trip tonight. They really are in it up to their necks. Lois and I were talking about going to the police. Heat of the moment, you know?"

"Who's Lois?" asked Trish.

Shelby proceeded to tell them about her meeting with Lois at O'Donnell's. She included every detail she could remember from the time she arrived at the pub to her last minutes with Lois, tucking her safely into a cab and sending her home.

"So Head Trip knew there was a possibility you could be injured?" Jake asked.

Shelby nodded. "Me and anyone else who takes a virtual vacation with them."

"And they used my image because they were trying to save a buck?" Trish was obviously disgusted.

"Yeah, I guess old Andrew wanted to show the feds he was running a squeaky-clean, by-the-book kind of business. I think he cut a lot of corners to get that contract, and now people are getting hurt. Asshole."

"Agreed, so let's just see how Andrew looks to his government buddies after I get done with him." Trish set her glass down. "I'm going to head back home and start cleaning up. Then tomorrow I'm going to start pushing until I get something concrete on Weasel Boy, and then I'm going to sit back and watch his little virtual world come crashing in on him. Do you think Lois will testify against him? At least tell the D.A. what she knows?"

"It'll take some persuasion. She's scared, but I think she'll do the right thing. I'll call her tomorrow. Listen, Trish, why don't you let us take you home? You could probably use some help cleaning up, and I feel responsible for your place getting tossed anyway."

"Why on earth do you feel responsible?"

"If it hadn't been for them using your image in my vacation—"

"Then they would have used it in someone else's. At least you're cute."

Trish's words dropped into the room like a pebble into smooth water. Shelby could feel her eyes getting bigger and watched as a flush of pink crept up from Trish's collar to the roots of her hair. She licked her lips and started to speak, but Jake broke the silence.

"Okay, girls, I like to clean a trashed apartment as much as the next guy, but I don't know if it's safe for you to be there. Everyone could just stay here. It could be like a slumber party. I'll pop popcorn. You guys can do each other's hair. It'll be great."

Trish laughed as she slipped off her stool. "That does sound like fun, I have to admit, but it's probably safer at my place than it is here. They've already been there and gotten what they wanted. They aren't coming back tonight. The police have put an extra patrol unit on the block. They'd have to be stupid to come back, and I think we've already determined they aren't stupid." She turned to Shelby. "So yeah, I'd love the help if you're still offering. I know it's late, but I don't think I'll be going to sleep anytime soon. My car's parked on the street. We could all pile in. I live close to the El so you can get to work in the morning. I mean, if you still want to."

Shelby's insides felt squishy. She was having a hard time not staring at Trish in a completely obvious way. Between clandestine meetings, robbery, and beautiful women, she was having trouble keeping her adrenaline in check.

She is a handsome woman, indeed, Shelby Hutchinson.

Very funny, Tasha. She looks exactly like you.

Yes, I know.

"Shel, you with us?" asked Jake.

"Yeah, sure, just foggy." She caught Jake's eye and recognized the look she got every time she drifted off into Tashaland. "Let's go."

Shelby's only personal contact with crime was from the shows she watched on television. In those, the detectives were strong, smart, and solved the crime in an hour. When she looked at the disaster that was Trish's apartment, she wondered how anyone could ever find anything in the mess that could be considered a clue. Broken glass littered the floor, couch cushions were strewn from the living room all the way down the hall. Every drawer in the kitchen had been emptied. Utensils lay like so many pickup sticks in the middle of the tile floor, covered in spilled food from the pantry, which also stood open. Over it all, the fine dark fingerprint powder used by the police had filtered onto everything. This was going to take more than an hour to clear up.

"Oh my God, Trish. I am so sorry."

Trish stepped over a broken picture frame and hung her coat in the closet by the front door. "You know what? It's okay. It'll get cleaned up. No use crying over spilled—everything." She gestured halfheartedly to her surroundings and let her hands fall to her sides.

Shelby's heart sank when she saw how resigned Trish looked, but who could blame her? Her entire life had been turned upside down in the course of a couple of days. Shelby could feel the beginnings of a headache and willed it away. She was not going to lose time to that now. She was going to help Trish clean up this mess, catch a couple hours of sleep, and then call Lois at Head Trip in the morning. She was not about to let that rat-faced loser Andrew get away with hurting innocent people any longer.

"Show me where they found your contract. Maybe they left something behind the police didn't notice."

"Sure, it was on my desk in my room. I had it out looking at it before we met with Andrew to see if I could use it against him. It's just back here." Trish led Shelby carefully through the living room and down the hallway to her bedroom.

Trish's bedroom looked like the same tornado had passed through. Papers littered her desktop and the floor. Bedside lamps were toppled; dresser drawers had been dumped. The bed itself was a ruin; the mattress showed deep slashes through the fabric all the way to the inner coils.

"I'll miss that bed." Trish sighed.

Shelby slipped an arm around Trish's shoulders. "Hey, you said it yourself. It'll get cleaned up. If you want, I'll help you shop for new stuff. I am a star shopper."

Trish leaned into Shelby. "I'll bet you are, and that would be great, but why don't we wait until Andrew is locked up in a tiny cage somewhere? I'd hate to get new stuff and have this happen all over again." Trish stopped leaning, which was too bad because Shelby really liked how it felt. "Come on, you can look at the desk while I try to put my underwear drawer back together."

Careful not to disturb anything, Shelby crossed to the desk and righted the lamp that was lying on its side. She blew on the papers on the desk, trying to dislodge the fingerprint powder that covered everything. She began sorting through the papers, making stacks, and in the process began learning more and more about Trish Aronoff. For instance, most people didn't have all these papers. Most people kept their records on disk or online where they were safe. Trish certainly wasn't a Luddite; she had a computer, a mobile phone, all the trappings of modern life. What was with all the paper? She also had photos, not digital images on a photocube, but real photos. Shelby found it hard not to look at them as she sorted through the mess. There were pictures of a little girl with her parents, the same little girl with a smaller boy. The little girl had to be Trish. The eyes gave her away. There were pictures of Trish, older now, with another young woman. A sister? A friend? No, in general people don't kiss their friends like that. Shelby tucked the photo into the stack and kept sorting. She found Trish's racquet club membership, her diploma from grad school, but nothing she thought of as a clue.

"*Summa cum laude*, huh? Not bad."

"What? Oh that. Yeah, I was always a good student. How about you?"

Shelby shrugged. "Yeah, I did okay." She pushed back from the desk. "I'm not finding anything here. At least nothing I think doesn't belong here. Can I ask you a question?"

"Sure," answered Trish, back to folding and stuffing.

"Why all the paper? And how did Andrew know you would have a copy of your contract anyway? That was a lucky shot on his part, wasn't it?"

"Not really. I told him I wanted a hard copy as well as the copy he e-mailed me. So he knew I had one. In fact, he had much the same look on his face as you do now when I told him I wanted one. Do you know how many people in this country lose everything, and I mean everything, because their online records get hacked? Or they cheap out on software and their system crashes? I did a story about it for the magazine when I first started there. I've been backing my stuff up with hard copy ever since."

"The pictures?"

Trish smiled and rocked back on her heels. "The pictures are just nostalgia. My mom always thought the whole photography thing with film and chemical developing was like magic. She took most of them. She was always popping up at odd moments to take pictures of us. Sometimes her timing wasn't the greatest."

Shelby nodded, thinking back to the lip lock that had been captured on film. She wondered what Trish's mom had thought about that. "Well, I think I've introduced some order back into the chaos over here, but you may never be able to find anything again. I don't know. Why don't I help with the rest?"

Shelby and Trish hung clothes back on hangers and refilled the closet. They matched shoes and put them back in their boxes. They folded the duvet and stuffed the torn sheets in the trash. Finally, they put the mattress back on the bed just to clear the path.

"The broken glass will have to wait," said Trish. "I'm not going to cut my hands to ribbons trying to get it out of the carpet. I'll call a service in the morning. I think we've done everything we can in here."

"Wait a second," Shelby called from behind the closet door. She stepped out into the room and turned on the lamp on the bedside table. "I found this. I hope it's all intact." She handed

Trish a small wooden box that was scarred, but it appeared to be a result of age rather than vandalism.

"Oh, I nearly forgot about that. It was in my closet on the shelf. I hadn't thought they had found it. Where was it?" She took the box from Shelby and lifted the lid. One hinge was detached from the box, which Trish treated like glass.

"It was on its side between the wall and the shelving. Is everything okay?"

"No, dammit. My grandmother's ring is missing!"

"Wait, I'll check in the closet to make sure it didn't fall out when the box fell."

Shelby looked but found nothing. She didn't want to tell Trish and see that look of loss on her face again. When she stepped out of the closet, she didn't have to say a word.

"It isn't in there, is it?" Tears began to roll down Trish's face. "Goddamnit! I didn't do anything wrong. I didn't even take a freaking vacation with these people. They fucked up, not me. This is so unfair."

Shelby didn't know what the right thing to do was. So she did what felt right. She wrapped Trish in her arms and let her cry.

"It was my grandmother's wedding ring. It probably wasn't worth anything, except to me. I was hoping I could give it to someone someday. This has been the shittiest day!"

When Trish's shoulders stopped shaking, Shelby gently pushed her to arm's length. She wiped Trish's tears with her thumbs. "Tomorrow, I want you to call the police and tell them about the ring. It'll probably show up at a pawnshop or something. We'll find it." Shelby looked up in the general direction of the doorway. "You know, I think Jake must have worked some miracles in the kitchen."

"Why do you say that?" Trish sniffed and wiped her eyes with the sleeve of her shirt.

"'Cause I smell popcorn."

Jake had indeed worked miracles in the kitchen. The counters were no longer dusted with black residue. The pantry was restored, and the dishwasher hummed. Three enormous trash bags stood just outside the doorway to the kitchen, more evidence of Jake's miracle work. Jake stood next to the small island, bowl of popcorn in front of him, pouring three glasses of wine.

"Jake, you are a godsend." Shelby scooped up a glass and handed it to Trish.

"Wow, you really are. Thank you, both of you. I had actually entertained thoughts of just moving out rather than cleaning this place up. The kitchen looks better than it did before it got trashed."

Jake raised his glass. "Yeah, that's me. Jake Fraser, champion of damsels in distress and all around great guy."

Shelby and Trish raised their glasses in answer and then dug into the popcorn bowl.

"You're lucky in one way, Trish," Jake mumbled through a mouthful of popcorn.

"How's that?" Trish answered.

"At least your living room and dining room have wood floors. I don't think it'll take too much to get them back in shape. How about your bedroom?"

"It's a total loss. The bed is ruined. The carpet is full of glass. I hope you're right about the living room being easily fixable because that's where we're going to be bunking tonight."

Shelby took a step backward and leaned out of the kitchen to survey the living room. Maybe it wasn't the ruin that Trish's bedroom was, but it would still be some time before any of them got any sleep.

❖

When she finally awoke, it was to the sound of Jake's snoring from across the room. Bright light poured in through the sliding glass door. Where was she? She was stiff and sore, that much was sure. She took a quick inventory. She was lying on the couch with her feet still in their sneakers, and her head was in someone's lap. Well, it wasn't Jake's because he was sprawled happily in the recliner. Which meant it was Trish's lap, and that was okay with her. She thought about closing her eyes and going back to sleep, but Trish shifted and Shelby became aware of just how much sunlight was streaming through the door. Carefully, she sat up, trying not to disturb Trish, whose head lolled on the back of the couch. Shelby got up and then eased Trish down on the couch and covered her with an afghan.

Shelby tiptoed into the kitchen and put a pot of coffee on then checked the time.

"Holy crap!" It was after noon. The last time she had looked at the clock it was about 4:30 a.m. She never slept this much. She quickly phoned in to work to let them know Jake was working on a special project from home for her and then wandered down the hall to the bathroom. Shelby didn't like what she saw in the mirror.

You are not looking so well, Shelby Hutchinson.

"Tell me something I don't know, Tasha." Shelby rubbed her face with both hands. It didn't help.

You don't know how you will find Trish's ring. You don't know how you will defeat your enemies at this Head Trip place.

"Wow, thanks for that."

The knock at the door startled Shelby into silence. "Shelby? Who are you talking to?" Oh, crap. It was Trish.

Shelby opened the door to see Trish holding two cups of coffee and wearing a concerned look on her face.

"Sorry, just talking to myself. I do that. You brought me coffee." She took the cup from Trish and took a tentative sip. "Mm. You do realize this makes you the perfect woman, don't you?" She closed her eyes and inhaled the rich, dark brew.

"I try."

Shelby realized what she had said and wondered if it was

safe to open her eyes. Flirting with a woman who had just been robbed was pretty low, but then she couldn't just stand here, eyes closed, looking like a doofus, so she opened her eyes and saw the half-smile on Trish's face. "You succeed," she said in an almost whisper before clearing her throat. "Is Jake up yet?"

"Nope, snoring away. I hope you don't mind. I ordered us a little breakfast—I guess lunch is more accurate—from the cantina down the block. They deliver, and I figured we could use it. I don't know about you, but I'm starving."

"That sounds great. You know, other than that great big lump over there that is Jake, this place looks pretty good, considering."

"Yeah, I think we made a great team last night. I still can't thank you enough."

The doorbell rang and Shelby said, "Breakfast is a good start."

They woke Jake, who joined them for an enormous breakfast of chorizo and eggs before heading off to his apartment. Shelby pushed away from the table and resisted the urge to lick her fingers.

"That was so good. Thank you."

"You are most welcome. I eat there all the time so they take good care of me." Trish shrugged and smiled.

"You eat there all the time? How is it that your ass isn't huge? I mean, wow, that didn't come out quite right."

Trish laughed. "That's okay. I play a lot of racquetball just so I can eat like this." She stood and started clearing plates. "What's next on the Head Trip agenda?"

Neither of them had mentioned Head Trip until this. It had been too nice a day to ruin with thoughts of Andrew and his bloodsucking greed. Shelby sighed.

"Now that it's past lunchtime, I think I'll call Lois and see if I can talk her into meeting me later. Maybe in daylight, maybe at the police station. I think it's time to stop the cloak-and-dagger bullshit and just go after Andrew."

"I think you're right. Whether Lois decides to go to the police or not, maybe you would be willing to go with me? I am going to go tell them about my grandmother's ring and the contract. I think this is way too big for us to handle alone or with just my attorney. This is definitely a police matter."

Shelby was relieved to hear that. As much as she loved her spy games, this one was real, and she had discovered recently real was more dangerous than make believe by far. "Okay then, let me call Lois and see how persuasive I can be."

She retrieved her phone from her pocket and dialed the Head Trip number.

"Head Trip Travel Services. Where would you like to go today?"

"Hello, I'd like to speak with Lois Evans, please."

There was no reply. Shelby looked at her phone to make sure she was still connected.

"Hello?"

"I'm sorry. Ms. Evans is not in."

The voice on the phone was shaking. What was going on here?

"But she asked me to call her this afternoon. Are you sure she isn't in?"

The voice lowered to a painful whisper. "Yes, ma'am. Lois was killed in an automobile accident last night. We're all just devastated, but maybe there is someone else who could help you?"

"No. No thank you. I'm sorry for your loss." Shelby stood stock-still. What had happened to Lois? Had she buckled her seat belt in the cab? Shelby felt a hand on her shoulder.

"Shelby, what is it?"

"Lois is dead. There was a car accident."

"Oh my God. I'm so sorry."

Shelby sank into the dining room chair. "I hardly knew her at all, but I thought putting her in the cab was the right thing to do. She had had a few drinks. She was upset because of this whole Andrew mess. She was scared, and I thought a cab was the way to go."

"Listen to me. You are not responsible for this. It was an accident. If you hadn't put her in the cab, she could have killed someone and herself. Do you know where it happened?"

"No, but we were at O'Donnell's on McClaren and I gave her address to the cabbie. So it had to be somewhere in between there."

Trish retrieved a pad of paper and a pen from the kitchen and pulled out her own phone. "Here's what we're going to do. Write down Lois's address for me. I will call my office and get in touch with Hannah. She handles the police beat. She'll look into this a bit and see what happened. Meanwhile, you go get in the shower. My robe is on the back of the door. Towels are under the sink."

"I remember," murmured Shelby. This was all getting to be too much. Maybe if she went back to sleep, she would wake up and none of this would be real. No Lois, no robbery, no Head Trip, no seizures, no Tasha, no Trish?

You would not like that so much, Shelby Hutchinson. You would miss me.

"I don't think so, Tasha."

"What?" asked Trish.

"Nothing. I think a shower is a good idea. I'll be out in a few."

Shelby left Trish to her phone calls and shuffled down the hall to Trish's bedroom. Before heading for the bathroom, she rummaged around until she found a pair of sweats and a T-shirt in one of Trish's drawers. Checking the sizes, she made a mental note to take up racquetball, dropped the clothes on the bed, and went on to the bathroom.

She turned the water up as hot as she could stand it and stood under the spray, letting the heat work on the knots in her neck and shoulders. About the time she had decided to reach for the soap, she realized she was crying and then she couldn't stop. She cried for Lois. She cried for Trish. She cried for herself. She even cried for the comatose climber. She cried until the water became uncomfortably cool then she quickly soaped her hair and body, rinsed off in the now-freezing water, and stepped out of the shower. Her feet sank into the cushy bath mat as she toweled off and dried her hair until it stood out in damp spikes all over her head. Shelby wrapped herself in Trish's robe and opened the bathroom door.

"Watch your step." Trish sat on the edge of the bed. Shelby wondered how long she had been sitting there and just how loudly she had been crying. "Broken glass. Don't cut yourself."

Shelby was keenly aware of how naked she was under the robe. "What's up?"

"I talked with Hannah at work. She looked into Lois's accident for us."

"And?"

"And the accident happened out on the west side loop. She took a turn too sharply and careened off the ramp. The car burst into flame. The identification was by dental record. They're waiting on toxicology reports, but the police believe alcohol was involved because there was an empty bottle of vodka in the car."

"I don't understand. She didn't have her car. I put her in a cab. I gave you the address. She lived on the other side of town."

"Maybe she decided she was okay to drive and had the cabbie take her back to the pub. Maybe she picked up the car and had the accident after that."

"But that's completely the wrong direction."

"She was drunk, Shelby. She got turned around. Or maybe she was on her way out of town, running away. You said she was scared."

Shelby started pulling clothes on under the robe. "She wasn't that drunk."

"But the bottle in the car—"

"Could have been put there by anyone. It could have been full, but the fire would have evaporated all the vodka. Besides, she wasn't drinking vodka. She was drinking scotch at the pub.

It's just too weird and too damn convenient for Andrew. Do you know where she is?"

Trish nodded. "She's at Northwestern."

Shelby smiled. She knew that was weird, but she was done crying. "How do you feel about a little trip to the morgue?"

"Is that a serious question?"

❖

After a quick stop at Shelby's apartment to retrieve her ID badge, Shelby had Trish park in the visitor lot near the emergency room of the hospital. If it all worked as she had planned, they would be in and out of the building without ever coming near any of her co-workers on the fifth floor. Because she worked in the IT department, her badge gave her access to almost any door in the place. They grabbed the elevator just inside the doors, and Shelby pushed the button for the basement.

"Oh my God, it's really in the basement, just like in the movies?" asked Trish.

"Well, yeah. It's quiet down here. No traffic. You can't have a lot of people running into the morgue on their way to obstetrics. Bad for business. I thought you had contacts in this hospital?"

"I do, but I don't write stories about death and murder. I write about doctors abusing prescription medication or nurses scheduled for so many shifts it affects patient care. I've never been anywhere near the morgue."

They stopped in front of a large set of double doors. Shelby passed her badge in front of the reader and the doors opened with a mechanical whoosh.

"You have now. Welcome to the hereafter."

"God, you have a weird sense of humor."

"Yeah, sorry. I think it's my version of whistling in the graveyard. You can't work in a hospital for any length of time without developing some kind of defense mechanism about death. Come on over here."

Shelby led Trish into a large room of gleaming tile and bright light with a bank of small doors on one wall. Several hospital gurneys and metal carts took up the middle of the room, and a desk sat on the opposite side near another door. Shelby made a beeline for the desk and the computer sitting on it. She entered her pass code into the computer.

"Excuse me. Can I help you?" The voice was almost menacing but quickly changed. "Oh, Shelby, it's you. I hadn't realized you were back at work. Are you feeling better, then?"

Shelby wheeled the desk chair away from the desk and turned to face the newcomer. "I am feeling better, Dr. Horvath, thanks, but I'm not back at work yet. I'm here for personal reasons."

"Personal reasons? And who is this?"

"Oh, I'm sorry," said Shelby. "This is my friend Trish Aronoff. She came with me as emotional support. You see, another friend of mine—Lois Evans—was killed in an MVA last night, and I came because I knew they brought her here."

Dr. Horvath put a heavy hand on Shelby's shoulder. "I am so sorry for your loss, Shelby, but all you had to do was call. I could answer any questions for you. You know that. You don't want to see her. There was a fire, and we had to use dental records for the identification of the remains."

A horrible image flashed through Shelby's head and with it a pinpoint of pain just behind her forehead. "So you're sure then that it was Lois?"

"I'm afraid so. Were you close?"

"We were pretty close. In fact, I saw her last night. The police mentioned they thought alcohol was involved. That wasn't like her at all." Shelby saw Trish's eyes go wide. She was fishing and tried to send Trish a mental message to just play along.

Dr. Horvath seated himself at the computer and pulled up a file. "Well, we won't know for certain until the tox screen comes back. If it gives you any consolation, she didn't suffer. She was killed instantly by the impact, massive head trauma."

Shelby flinched and the pain in her head bloomed.

"I apologize, Shelby, and to you, Miss Aronoff. I'm not always the most tactful person when it comes to death. Is there anything else I can do for you?"

"Could I see her effects? Um, I guess I just need to see something concrete to make this real. Since I can't see her body."

"I don't know, Shelby. Her next of kin haven't been notified yet. It's against procedure."

It was the tear rolling down her face and splashing to the shiny tile floor that did it.

"Okay, I don't see what harm there is." Dr. Horvath opened the top drawer of a file cabinet near his desk and pulled out a manila envelope. He handed it to Shelby. "I'll give you a bit of privacy. Just leave the envelope on the desk when you're done. Again, I am truly sorry for your loss. It was nice meeting you, Miss Aronoff."

Dr. Horvath disappeared back through the door he had come in, leaving Shelby and Trish staring at one another, the envelope between them.

"Wow, are you good! You had him eating out of your hands."

"He's a sweet man," said Shelby. "I don't think I laid it on too thick, did I? I don't want him to never trust me again. I just want to see what's in this bag." She cleared a spot on the small desk and dumped out the contents of the envelope.

"Why do you want to see what's in there so much? What's it going to tell you?"

"I have no idea, but I just can't believe Lois went back for her car, drank an entire bottle of vodka, and then decided to leave town. Let's see, one badly scorched wallet."

She handed the wallet to Trish who carefully opened it to reveal an almost destroyed driver's license. "She was pretty, I think."

"Yes," said Shelby. "She was, and young and scared, and she sure as hell didn't deserve this. Here's a compact, I think. It looks like it had lip gloss or something in it. There's a lip brush with it. Her cell phone and two rings. Dammit! There's nothing—"

"Oh my God!" Trish clutched her arm.

"What is it?"

"The ring, the little one." Trish pointed a shaking finger toward the item on the table. "It's my grandmother's."

Shelby picked up the ring from the desk and held it up to the light. "Are you sure?"

Trish nodded, her eyes welling.

"Okay then." She closed her hand around the ring and pushed it into the pocket of her sweats. As quickly as she could, she scooped up the remainder of Lois's belongings and dropped them back into their envelope. A thought tickled the back of Shelby's brain and she reached back into the envelope and retrieved one more item. Then she set the envelope on the desk without another glance and grabbed Trish's hand. "Let's get out of here."

They were out of the morgue and through the security doors before either of them spoke. "What just happened, Shelby?"

Shelby reached into her pocket and pulled out the ring. She took Trish's hand and placed the ring in her palm. "It's yours. You should have it back."

"I know it's mine, but why was it here and why was it with Lois?"

The elevator arrived and Shelby got in with Trish right behind her. She punched the button for the first floor as fast as she could. She wanted out of this hospital and somewhere she could think.

"There's only one thing it could mean. The people who trashed your apartment, stole your contract and your ring are the same people who made sure Lois had an accident. They planted the ring on her or in her car to connect her to the burglary. I'm not sure why. To make her look like some sort of disgruntled, crazy employee or to scare the crap out of us. I can't quite figure it out."

The bell chimed as they reached their floor and the elevator doors slid open.

"Do you hear that?" asked Shelby.

"What the elevator chime?"

"No, that buzzing. It makes my head hurt." The buzz in Shelby's ears grew deafening and her vision blurred. The hospital emergency room looked like she was seeing it through a fish-eye lens. She tried to say something but all she could hear was the buzzing and Tasha.

You are having trouble now, Shelby Hutchinson. It's very bad trouble.

CHAPTER TWELVE

*W*ake up, Shelby Hutchinson! Wake up now! You must fight for your life!

It was hard to breathe. And hot, so hot. Everything hurt, but if Shelby just went to sleep, it wouldn't hurt so much.

Shelby Hutchinson! GET UP NOW! Or you really will be a dead thing.

"Fuck you, Tasha, let me sleep."

"Shut up, you little bitch, and die already!"

That wasn't Tasha's voice. Adrenaline flooded Shelby's body as she realized the reason it was so hard to breathe was that there was a hospital-issue pillow being held over her face. She began to push and struggle against her assailant. Panic was building in every inch of her body.

Lie still. Pretend to be dead. You must be ready to move quickly.

Shelby did as she was told. It took all her willpower to stop struggling and play dead. But Tasha was right. As soon as she stopped, the pressure of the pillow eased. She didn't dare take the huge breath of air she wanted. She waited, lungs burning. When the pillow began to move away from her face, Shelby sprang into action. She curled onto her side and rolled away from her attacker, wincing in pain as the IV in her arm jerked free. She landed lightly on her feet and shoved the IV pole at her surprised assailant, hitting him hard in the face. He went down in a heap, breathing heavily. As he struggled to get back on his feet, she heard Tasha's voice in her head again.

Study him, Shelby Hutchinson. Remember him. Look for weakness.

"Weakness? What the fuck, Tasha?" But study him she did. Bleached blond hair, dark brown eyes, hollow, menacing scowl, black leather coat, huge cut on his forehead. As he struggled to get up from the floor, Shelby saw his hand disappear into the recesses of his coat and reemerge with something that caught the light as he turned it over. "Oh, fuck, Tasha. He's got a knife."

And you have a hospital bed. Use it.

"Oh, yeah." She shoved the wheeled bed at her assailant. He went down for a second time.

Finish him, Shelby Hutchinson.

Shelby came around to his side of the bed and grabbed a metal tray from her bedside. She took her best batting stance and swung the metal tray at his head. The tray hit home with a resonant clang, the impact vibrating up her arms; her attacker crumpled to the floor. Without another thought, Shelby dropped the now-dented tray on top of him and scooped up her bag of belongings as she ran out of her room.

She definitely wasn't in the ER anymore. It was too quiet. Her survival instincts completely engaged, Shelby scanned the hallway. At the end of the hallway, her ticket to freedom glowed in the dim lighting—the exit sign pointing toward the stairwell. With a final glance behind her, Shelby took off down the hall for the exit. She pushed into the stairwell and started to climb.

What are you doing, Shelby Hutchinson? You must go back. You must finish him off or get out of this building. It could be a trap for you.

"I'm going up to my office, Tasha. I don't know who the hell that was down there or who's in on this, but I know Jake isn't. Jake will help me. Besides, I'm not running out into the street with my bare ass hanging out of this hospital gown!"

When she reached the fifth floor, Shelby stopped at the door to listen and catch her breath. She gathered her thoughts and the back of her gown and stepped through the door with as much dignity as she could muster, which wasn't easy considering she was barefoot and basically naked. The IT department hummed along in its usual way, and fortunately for Shelby, that meant most of her co-workers were busy behind their own doors. She backed into her office and leaned her forehead against the door.

"Hey, nice view there, Shel. What the hell are you doing up here?"

Shelby clutched at the back of her hospital gown and spun around. "Shit, Jake. Scare me to death, why don't you? It's not enough that some goon is trying to smother me with a pillow. Now I need to worry about my best friend doing me in? Why are you in here?" She pulled her clothes out of the plastic bag.

"What do you mean someone tried to smother you? I'm calling security."

"No, you're not. Put the phone down." She slipped her jeans on under her gown, which made her instantly feel a good bit more in charge. "I need you to fill me in on what happened, and then you've got to get me out of here—to your apartment, I think—and then we've got to make some serious decisions, and I've got to call Trish. Start with what day is this and why was I in the ER?"

"It's Saturday, Shelby. You had a seizure in the morgue yesterday, so they wanted to keep you here for the night. I convinced them to let you sleep it off in a quiet spot in the ER. Since we talked about it last week, I knew that you wanted the seizure thing kept on the down-low at work, and I did some home computer work for one of the docs and he owed me a favor." Jake looked at Shelby and scratched his head. "Which leads me to the question, how did you get up here, and what the hell do you mean someone was trying to smother you?"

"I have no fucking clue. I was sleeping and then I wasn't

because some bleach blond hired thug guy came after me. Good thing someone was around to help me."

"Who helped you?"

"Tasha did. She woke me up. I heard her as plain as I hear you right now. She told me to wake up, and when I did, some guy was holding a pillow over my face. I fought him off and clocked him with a tray, then I came up here. I hoped that you might know what was going on and be able to help me."

"Well, of course I'll try, but I still think we should call security."

"No, I don't want anyone to know where I am except you and Trish. Wait a minute. I've been out since yesterday? Have you talked to her? Is she okay?"

"As far as I know. I had to send her home last night. She didn't want to leave."

Shelby smiled and felt her insides get fuzzy and warm. She pulled her sweater over her head and pushed to her feet. "So I had a seizure in the morgue? I remember Trish was there. We'd been down there to check on Lois. Poor Lois. I remember coming off the elevator and everything went wonky. Then nothing until I heard Tasha yelling at me to wake up. She saved my life. I guess that makes up for shooting me. Sort of." Shelby shook her head. "Grab your stuff and let's get to your place. I'll feel a lot better once I'm there. We can call Trish on the way."

"The car's on the second level of the parking garage as always."

"Lead on, Macduff."

❖

Shelby called Trish from the car on the way to Jake's apartment.

"Hello?"

"Trish? It's Shelby. I need you to meet me at Jake's right now."

"You're out of the hospital? What are you talking about? I don't understand."

"Long story, and I will tell you when you get to Jake's. I know you're at work, but you need to get out of there and meet us. Don't worry too much. I'm fine, and Jake tells me you wanted to stay with me last night. That means a lot." Jake cleared his throat, a reminder to Shelby she wasn't alone. "We'll be there in about five minutes. Try to make sure you aren't followed."

"Followed? What's going on, Shelby? You're scaring me."

"I'm sorry. I just want you to be careful. I'll explain everything when you get there." Shelby wondered exactly how she was supposed to explain something she didn't understand herself.

CHAPTER THIRTEEN

When they arrived at Jake's apartment, Shelby headed straight for the bathroom to at least try to wash up a little. Being in the ER always made her feel grubby.

Da, like sleeping in a hayloft, Shelby Hutchinson?

She stared at the mirror. "Very funny, Tasha." But she also wasn't going to admit that Tasha was right, so she quit looking at the dark circles under her eyes and peeled off her sweater. As she splashed some water on her face and scrubbed soap over the ache in her arm where her IV had been pulled out, she replayed the attack in her head trying to remember if she had ever seen her assailant before. Nothing registered, but she had a sneaking suspicion he was being paid by Andrew. Shelby got a little shaky when she thought about what would have happened if Tasha hadn't awakened her.

"Sorry I was snippy about the hayloft remark. Thank you, Tasha. Thank you for saving my life."

You are welcome, Shelby Hutchinson. Now you must find this Andrew and make him suffer for what he has done. He will not stop coming after you until you are dead.

"Yeah, I was afraid of that. And not just me. He'll try to kill Trish too, but I honestly don't know what to do. I only have suspicions, no real evidence the police would take seriously. I'm sure Andrew is good at covering his tracks. He probably already has everything hidden away. The police will never find anything, and then I'll look like an idiot. Then I'll be a dead idiot."

You disappoint me, Shelby Hutchinson. I taught you many things. I know you learned them because you did very well against the man at the hospital. Now you need to think like me. Stop being a good girl. Police! Bah! They cannot help you, as you say. You must help yourself and your beautiful lady friend.

Shelby twisted the faucets off and stepped out of the shower. She wrapped a towel around her hair and bundled herself into Jake's terrycloth robe. "I think you're right, Tasha. No more Ms. Nice Guy."

Shelby left the bathroom and wandered out to Jake's living room, toweling her hair dry.

"Hi, Shelby. It's good to see you."

"Trish, hi. It's good to see you too." Shelby wanted to race across the room and hug Trish, but her feet felt rooted to the carpet. Fortunately, Trish didn't seem to have the same problem. She went to Shelby and pulled her into a warm embrace.

"I was scared for you. The doctors didn't know what to do."

"Hey, it's okay. I'm fine, really. Thank you for hanging in there with me."

"Hello, you two, I was there too."

Shelby laughed. "Of course you were. I saw you today in my office. You were just waiting for me to kick the bucket so you could take over."

"Yeah, well, that's not funny. You came way too close today."

"What happened?" asked Trish.

Shelby took Trish by the hand and sat on the couch. "I woke up this afternoon with some skinny Billy Idol wannabe trying to smother me with a hospital pillow. I managed to fight him off and whack him in the head with a metal tray. Then I grabbed my clothes and went upstairs to find Jake. That's all I know except I'd bet my last dime that the wannabe was sent by Andrew."

"What do we do now? I don't think we have anything tangible to take to the police. They're going to ask a lot of questions like why you left the hospital if someone attacked you. I'm afraid they just might think all of this has something to do with your seizures, and if Andrew has locked down Head Trip as tightly as Lois said, there may not be anything for the police to find there even if we could get a warrant issued to examine their computer records."

Shelby listened carefully to what Trish was saying and knew in her heart she was right. If she went to the police, they would probably dismiss her as at best someone with neurological impairment and at worst a whack job. And heck, they didn't even know she had a Russian spy living in her head. What could they do? She remembered Tasha telling her to think like she did, and a plan began to develop in her brain.

"You make some good points, and I think we've been going about this all wrong. We've been completely reactive, just responding to the curves Andrew keeps throwing at us. Isn't it time we stepped up and made the first move?"

Jake and Trish looked at her expectantly.

"My guess is Andrew is feeling pretty confident. He thinks he has both of us running scared. Hell, he may think I'm completely out of the way. He got rid of Lois. He's sealed off Head Trip. He probably has his files hidden under several layers of encryption. It's a good thing I know a thing or two about computers."

"I don't like where I think you're headed with this," said Jake.

Trish looked at Jake. "What? Where is she going?"

"It's where *we* are going. We're going back to Head Trip, and I am going to do a little digging. Andrew has to have left a trail, and if we're lucky that trail might lead to some kind of treatment for whatever it is that has happened to me."

Trish took one of Shelby's hands in her own. "Shelby, you can't just waltz in there and start fooling around with their computers, and I don't think Andrew will fall for the three of us disguised as, I don't know, plumbers or something. Plus, Lois is gone. She can't get us in. How are you planning to do this?"

"You forget, both of you, that Head Trip gave me the opportunity to learn how to be a spy. Whatever Tasha was, she taught a heck of a lesson." Shelby's face started to get hot. She took a deep breath and willed it down. "A little breaking and entering will be a snap." She had to laugh when she saw the looks on their faces. Jake knew her too well. He probably wasn't that surprised. Trish, on the other hand, looked like she couldn't quite believe what she had just heard.

She does not know you well yet, Shelby Hutchinson, but I think she is impressed.

I don't know if I would go that far, Tasha.

"Shelby, breaking and entering! Are you—"

"Nuts? Probably. Look, Trish, we've played by the rules because that's what normal people do. Where has that gotten us? This is not a normal situation. This is not a Better Business Bureau kind of problem. This is rat-faced Andrew not giving a shit who he hurts to make a fortune. He's in it up to his neck, and getting rid of us, of Lois, just isn't a big deal to him evidently. Andrew doesn't play by any rules other than the ones he has made for himself. It's time to make him play by our rules."

Shelby studied Trish's face. She wanted to see trust. She wanted to see belief, but all she could see was fear and confusion. Right now she needed Trish to be Tasha, and that just wasn't happening. Well, she would have to be Tasha for both of them.

"Jake, where's the stuff that was in my pants pockets?"

"There was an envelope in the hospital bag. I'll get it for you."

Shelby knew she was smiling a little too brightly. Trish probably did think she was crazy, but it felt so damn good to be *doing* something. "Trish, I'm sorry. I don't mean to scare you, and if you don't want to go with me, I'll understand. It's just that I feel like a huge part of my life has been stolen from me. I don't know if I'll ever stop having these seizures, if I'll ever stop seeing

Tasha pointing that gun at me and firing. I know how violated you said you felt because Head Trip had used your image without permission. Imagine how I feel."

"Oh, Shelby! I never for a minute compared what happened to me to your situation."

"I know that. I just mean I can't sit and do nothing. Andrew won't stop until he makes sure that no one finds out about the problems with Head Trip. That's the only way he'll be safe from losing all his government contracts and private clients."

"And he won't be safe until we are out of the way."

"Exactly." Jake handed Shelby the envelope of her belongings, which she slit open with her thumb. "Here it is."

"Here what is?" Jake asked.

Shelby handed him the scorched security badge that had belonged to Lois. "Our ticket into Head Trip. Do you think you could duplicate this, Jake?"

He turned the card over in his hands, examining it closely. "Probably. It's just a simple strip like on a credit card. Our badges at the hospital are similar, though honestly more sophisticated. But I thought you said Andrew had locked Head Trip down and changed Lois's security access."

"To the computer system, yes, but Lois said everyone still went in to work. I'm guessing that the badge still works. Maybe he canceled her access after he killed her, but he had other things to worry about like offing me. My guess is he never bothered to do it because of the fiery car crash. He wouldn't even know that the badge still existed."

A slow smile spread across Jake's face. "Aren't you the devious one? Yeah, give me a couple hours and I can do something with this as long as the strip will still read, but I'll have to go back to the office. There's bound to be questions about where you are. What do you want me to say?"

"Tell them I went home, and check and see if a spiky-haired guy with a big knot on his head showed up for treatment. My guess is he got out of there quick, but you never know."

Jake pocketed the badge and pulled his coat on. "I'll call you as soon as I know something. I take it you want to move on this quickly?"

"Tonight if we can do it, Jake. Thank you."

The door clicked shut behind him, leaving Shelby and Trish alone. The apartment seemed unnaturally quiet after all the excitement of just a few moments before. Shelby looked at Trish, saw her beauty, her vulnerability, and felt her newfound bravado fading. Beautiful women had always made her nervous. It didn't help that in this case she had known this particular beautiful woman intimately, even if it hadn't really been her. God, that sounded stupid even in her own head.

"Still plotting against evil Andrew?" Trish asked.

Shelby felt the heat rise in her cheeks. "Um no, actually I was just thinking about you. You're beautiful, you know?"

Trish looked down at her hands, then shoved them into the pockets of her jeans. "Thanks, you're sweet to say that."

Shelby took a step toward Trish. "I'm not trying to be sweet. I'm trying to be smooth. I'm just not very good at it."

Trish laughed and the tension in the room melted away. She opened her arms. "Come here. You don't have to be smooth. You just have to be you."

For a moment, Shelby wondered which "you" she was supposed to be. Shelby Hutchinson, IT Director? Shelby Hutchinson, victim? Shelby Hutchinson, secret agent? She stopped wondering when Trish wrapped her arms around her and kissed her. All the tension and heat came back in a rush as Shelby fell into the kiss. Trish's lips were as soft as she remembered from her vacation. She smelled fabulous and she tasted better. No trace of vodka this time. Shelby combed through Trish's hair with her fingers, resisting the urge to curl her fingers into fists.

Trish pulled back, breathing hard and licking her lips. "This is crazy. You just got out of the hospital. Someone tried to kill you."

"That's why this isn't crazy. I could have died. This makes me feel alive."

Trish stepped back farther and turned away from Shelby. She smoothed her hands down her jeans. "But is it about me? Or is it about, you know, the other me? Tasha?"

Shelby came up from behind Trish and put her hands on her shoulders. "Tasha isn't real," she said. "Tasha is someone Head Trip planted in my head. You are real and you are beautiful and I have wanted you, well, not from the first moment I saw you because you seriously scared the crap out of me, but from pretty soon after that. It's just all been so crazy. It's hard to date someone when you never know when a seizure will strike or when some greedy bastard will try to kill you."

Trish turned and put her arms around Shelby. "Shelby, shut up and kiss me again."

Shelby obliged, once again feeling the heat of their kiss suffusing her whole being. She backed Trish toward the couch and sat down, pulling her onto her lap. Shelby stroked up and down the length of Trish's spine, stopping at the top of the waistband of her jeans. She ran her hand around to the front and slipped under Trish's sweater. Trish's silky skin yielded under Shelby's touch. She continued to explore, pushing upward until her fingertips grazed the lace of Trish's bra. Trish shuddered and leaned into Shelby's touch.

"God, Shelby, touch me, please."

Shelby reached behind Trish and unhooked her bra then gently shifted her off her lap and onto her back on the couch. She stopped for a moment to look at Trish, really look at her. There was no sign of Tasha around Trish's intense blue eyes. Nothing harsh or cold or calculating in the set of her jaw. Shelby rubbed her thumb across Trish's full lower lip.

No, Shelby Hutchinson, she is not me. You must be careful with her, keep her safe.

Shelby squeezed her eyes closed.

"Are you okay, Shelby? Is it your head?"

"No, it's nothing. I want to touch you." Shelby pushed Trish's sweater and bra up, and Trish leaned up to pull them the rest of the way off. When she settled back against the couch cushions, Shelby was once again struck by her loveliness. She lowered herself to cover Trish. She captured her lower lip between her teeth and teased then nibbled then teased some more, running her tongue across Trish's teeth.

Trish pulled Shelby closer, taking control of the kiss, but Shelby was having none of it. She pulled Trish's hands from around her neck and pushed them up until Trish's arms were over her head.

"Leave them there," she whispered, her voice husky. Shelby slid down Trish's body, her hands stroking. She took her time getting to know Trish's skin, the curve of her flesh. She noted the amount of pressure it took to make Trish's nipples rise beneath her hands, felt the quickening of Trish's breath as her mouth trailed from collarbone across the swell of her breast. Shelby smiled at Trish's small squeal as she took first one nipple then the other into her mouth. She wanted to stay right there with the feel of Trish's nipple under her tongue for the rest of her life, but it had been so long. As much fun as the romp with Tasha had been, it hadn't been real, and this was so real. Shelby slid her hand over the soft curve of Trish's belly and unbuttoned her jeans. When the response to her unspoken question was met by a deep sigh, Shelby pushed forward, fingertips grazing soft curls. She teased with gentle tugs before cupping Trish in her hand, feeling the intense heat and wetness she had hoped to find.

"Take my pants off, please," Trish whispered with a hint of desperation.

Shelby didn't need to be asked twice. She rolled off the couch and knelt between Trish's knees to pull her jeans off. Shelby scooted down the couch onto her stomach and placed Trish's legs over her shoulders. It may have been a long time, but she hadn't forgotten this part. Gently, she stroked Trish's clit with her thumb until Trish raised her hips to meet her rhythm and then she replaced her thumb with her tongue. Trish gasped and Shelby felt her stiffen then relax back into the same hypnotic rhythm. Shelby licked and swirled and just as Trish's breath became ragged, she pushed two fingers into her, quickening the pace until Trish tumbled over the edge, her cunt convulsing around Shelby's fingers.

They lay tangled together for a few minutes, Shelby continuing to softly stroke Trish's skin. "You are amazing."

Trish laughed at that. "I think I should be saying that. Are you coming up here so I can return the favor?"

Shelby tried not to stiffen, but she was afraid. Afraid she would see Tasha again, hear Tasha again, or worst of all, say Tasha's name at an inopportune moment. She wanted Trish like she hadn't wanted anyone in a very long time, maybe ever, but she knew she had to wait until she could exorcise all her Head Trip demons. She scooted up the couch and pulled a blanket over both of them. She smoothed Trish's hair and kissed her.

"I really want you to return the favor, in a big way, but I don't think I'm ready yet. I will be. I know I will be, but right now, I'm scared. Can you understand?"

Tears welled in Trish's eyes, but she nodded. "I do understand. It's about Head Trip, all of it. You feel…broken isn't the right word."

"Yes, yes it is. Broken is exactly the word. I feel so completely out of control, and I have to get that back, but I wanted to touch you so much."

"Come here. We'll get through this and then you'll have to tie me up to keep me away from you." Trish pulled Shelby into a tight hug and snuggled under the blanket.

"That probably wouldn't keep either of us away, you know."

"I know."

Chapter Fourteen

Two hours later the apartment door slammed open.

"Shel! Oh shit, sorry!"

Shelby leapt off the couch, pulling the blanket with her and uncovering Trish. Shelby and Jake stared at each other for a moment before Shelby grabbed at the blanket and covered Trish, who was looking more than a little startled.

"Shel, I am so sorry, but I called and called. When you didn't answer, I ran home. I was scared shitless, but you're both okay, right?"

"We're fine," Trish said, as she wrapped the blanket around her and scooped up her clothes from where they had landed on the floor. "But if you'll excuse me for just a minute, I'll be right back." She shuffled out of the room toward the bathroom.

"Crap," Jake muttered.

His expression reminded Shelby of a wounded puppy. She felt bad.

"I'm so sorry. Is she okay? I wouldn't have just barged in if I had known."

"Jake, it's your apartment. She'll be fine. We fell asleep and I didn't hear the phone. So what did you find out about the security badge?"

Jake reached into his pocket, pulled out a badge, and handed it to Shelby. "There's no picture on it, but I didn't figure you would be checking in at the reception desk. Fortunately, there wasn't much damage to Lois's badge. It was scorched around the edges, a little melty, but the strip was still readable. I ran it through the machine at work and used one of the hospital's blanks. As long as Andrew didn't cancel her clearance, this should get you in."

Shelby turned the badge over in her hands, her mind racing a mile a minute at the possibilities. "Thanks, Jake."

"Did you get the badge to work?" Trish asked as she came back into the room.

Jake cleared his throat. "Yeah, I did, but I wish you guys would rethink this. Isn't there some way we can bring the police in on this? This plan—is there a plan? This plan is way too dangerous. If you could just sit down at the police station—"

"The police? Please." Shelby winced when she heard Tasha's words coming out of her own mouth. "We've been through this. All we have are suspicions, and I'm just not the most reliable witness at the moment given my medical issues. It has to be this way. I can get in to Head Trip with this." She held up the badge. "I'll find something. Andrew isn't as smart as he thinks he is. Then I'll get out. Maybe then we can go to the police. If nothing else, there has to be something about the rock climber, a cyber trail of some kind. Once I have that, we can shut Andrew's weaselly ass down."

"Wait a minute, Shelby. This sounds an awful lot like you're thinking of going in there alone."

"That's exactly what I'm talking about. You guys can keep an eye on the door for me, but there is no reason for anyone else to go in the building besides me."

"You can forget it. I'm not going to let you go in there by yourself. What if you have a seizure?" Trish was adamant.

"What she said, Shel."

Shelby stuffed the badge in her pocket and rolled her eyes. "What am I supposed to do with you two?"

You could knock both of them out. They are in the way.

"Yeah, like that would work." Shelby wandered into the

kitchen and pulled some juice from the refrigerator. "All right, if we're going to do this and you all insist on being a part of it, we need to be smart. I'll go in with Trish. Jake, you get to be lookout. Before you say anything, Andrew doesn't know you. If you're hanging around outside Head Trip—"

"I won't be recognized. I'm not very suspicious."

"That's what I am hoping for, yeah. Trish, do you still remember the layout of the offices?"

Trish nodded. "Sure. Are we heading back to Andrew's office?"

"Yep. Just as soon as the sun goes down, and let's hope this visit is a little more productive than the last one."

CHAPTER FIFTEEN

The car pulled to a stop, its tires crunching over sticks, broken glass, and other debris left behind by the street sweepers. Shelby tried to push the horror movie music out of her head. She had enough tension rolling through her body; she didn't need the soundtrack.

"That's it, Jake. We're close enough. Can you see the door?"

"Yeah, I can see it, but what if Andrew decides to use the back door, or what if he's still in there?"

"First of all, I don't think Andrew is a back door kind of guy. He thinks he's on top of the situation. He has Head Trip locked down tight. He thinks Trish is running scared, and he thinks I'm out of the way. Even if he knows by now I'm not out of the way, I'm sure the last thing he's thinking about me is that I'd even consider taking the fight to him." Shelby stopped and shook her head. "There's no need for him to be skulking around to the back door or be here after hours, for that matter. He's arrogant and that's what is going to get him caught. Let's go over this one more time and then get a move on. I don't want to be here any longer than absolutely necessary. Jake, stay here. Keep your eyes open. If anything, and I mean anything, looks funny, page me with the nine-one-one signal, and I'll get out of there. Trish, I'm still hoping I can talk you into staying in the car with Jake."

"Keep right on hoping. It won't do you any good. You're not going in that building alone."

Tell her you are not alone, Shelby Hutchinson. Tell her you have a badass Soviet agent going with you.

"Yeah, that's not going to happen."

"What's not going to happen, Shelby?"

"Um, I'm not going to get my way on this, am I?"

Trish pressed her lips together and forced a smile.

"Fine then, we go in together. Straight to Andrew's office. I'll tackle his computer, and since you insist on coming in with me, you can see about finding anything else. Start with his assistant's desk. Look for disks, portable storage drives, anything that we can take and look at later. We should be out of there in less than fifteen minutes."

Shelby had the sudden urge to have everyone synchronize their watches, but realized none of them were wearing one. This spy shit had been easier in her vacation. Except for that getting shot part, of course.

Shelby took a deep breath and opened the car door. The night was clear and cold in a way only Chicago can be. The air coming in off the lake was chilled like the perfect martini, and like the drink, it slowed you down, dulled your senses.

Shelby held the door for Trish, then poked her head back into the car. "We'll be back in a few. It'll be okay."

"I hope so," Jake answered. "Don't worry; I've got your back." He held up his phone and wiggled it.

Shelby gave him a final grin she hoped was more reassuring than she felt, then turned and headed for the front door of Head Trip. Even though there were other people on the street, all going about the business of their everyday lives, Shelby felt like all eyes were on her and Trish. It was as if they were glowing in the dark or had flashing neon signs hanging over their heads that proclaimed "about to commit a felony." She felt a hand slip into her pocket and squeeze hers.

"I'm scared, Shelby."

"Me too, but it'll work out. It has to."

They marched up the steps of the unassuming building that housed Head Trip and stopped at the front door. Shelby resisted the urge to wave and stick her tongue out at the security camera as she pulled Lois's badge from her pocket and slid it through the reader. When the green lights flashed and the door locks clicked, Shelby exhaled. For the briefest moment, she didn't know what to do next. Part of her had expected their plan would be stalled right here at the door.

"Come on, Shelby. Let's go."

Shelby pushed the door open and stepped into Head Trip's empty lobby. It was dark, but the security lights gave them enough illumination to see where they were going. Shelby let Trish take the lead while she followed behind, alert for any sign of trouble. They passed the reception desk, and Shelby used Lois's badge again to gain access to the rest of the office. Once through the door, Trish tugged on Shelby's sleeve.

"This way," she whispered, heading down a long hallway past rows of tiny cubicles. She couldn't help wondering which one had been Lois's.

It's no time for sadness. You are sharp, Shelby Hutchinson.

Tasha's reminder snapped Shelby back into the moment, but she found being on high alert was just making her more anxious. Who knew after hours buildings were so damn noisy? While their footsteps were muffled by the carpet, Shelby could hear the environmental controls humming, the fans on the extensive computer equipment blowing. Frankly, she would rather have had echoing silence to deal with. The sound of her footsteps and rapid heartbeat would have been fine compared to the background noises that filled her senses and made listening for anything else difficult.

They reached Andrew's assistant's desk and Trish edged her way around it toward the data storage cabinet.

"I'll get started here. Call me if you need anything."

Shelby had to admire Trish's attitude. She knew she had to

be scared. Hell, Shelby was practically terrified, but Trish was determined to see this through for her. The thought hit her like a wave. Trish was doing this for her.

"If you find anything, take it. We'll deal with the ramifications later. I just want to get out of here as fast as we can."

Shelby looked at Andrew's door, which stood slightly ajar. With a deep breath, she pushed through and headed for his desk. It was, of course, pristine—a clean wooden expanse with nary a pencil or paper clip to mar its perfect surface.

"Freak. No one is this neat."

She seated herself behind his desk and powered up his computer. "Password, schmassword, Andrew." Shelby turned on her best fake Russian accent. "We don't need no stinkin' password."

The desktop of Andrew's computer was as uncluttered as his actual desktop. It took Shelby a few moments to access his file structure and figure out how he named his files. "Who functions like this?" She continued to open and scan folders and documents. Finally, tucked away in several layers of subfolders, Shelby found what she had been looking for. In a folder named "Liabilities" she found information on the rock climber and every other person who had been injured by Head Trip's incompetence and Andrew's greed. As she scanned the folders, she found the one with her name on it, but let her finger hover over the mouse for just a second. She wasn't quite sure if she wanted to read what was in there or not, but curiosity got the better of her. She opened the file and scanned over what she already knew. On the last page of the file was a record of a funds transfer from Head Trip to a William Sanger in the amount of $2,000. The picture of William Sanger made Shelby's blood boil.

"Two thousand dollars! You only paid that spiky-haired idiot two grand to off me?" Shelby pulled a thumb drive from her pocket and inserted it into a port on the computer. "Shit, you could have saved yourself the money. William Sanger was a certified idiot and no match for someone who had learned to defend herself on one of your vacations."

She checked the time on her phone and silently urged the computer to move faster. A few more minutes and they could be out of there. "And then, Andrew, you are going to get what you deserve, you weasel-faced, neat freak, piece of crap."

"Now, now, Miss Hutchinson, is that any way to talk to the man holding your girlfriend at gunpoint?"

Shelby froze. When she lifted her eyes from the computer screen, Andrew was indeed holding Trish at gunpoint. He had her by the arm and the gun was pointed at the back of her ear.

"Shit."

"Indeed. Come out from behind the desk, Miss Hutchinson. Move very slowly."

In a move she hoped was hidden from Andrew, Shelby pulled the thumb drive from its port and let it drop to the floor.

"If you hurt her, Andrew, I will kill you."

"How noble, Miss Hutchinson. How brave, how incredibly stupid. I have the gun. You have nothing."

Nothing but Tasha. What do we do here, Tasha?

Wait, Shelby Hutchinson. You must wait for an opening. Right now you are screwing, yes?

"Screwed, but yeah, that's pretty much it."

Andrew laughed. "Yes, I would say you are definitely screwed, as you so eloquently put it. You are making my life infinitely more difficult. If it were just one of you, I could simply shoot you, call the police, and expose you for the intruder, the disgruntled client, the murderer you are."

"Murderer? What the hell are you talking about?"

"He means Lois," Trish said. "That's why you planted my ring, isn't it?"

"Yes. That didn't go exactly as planned. And William evidently didn't do his job either."

"No duh. You only paid him two thousand dollars, you idiot.

What did you expect? You get what you pay for. Why are you here? Don't tell me this is all some happy little coincidence."

Andrew laughed again, and Shelby noticed his hand loosening its grip ever so slightly on Trish's upper arm. She caught Trish's eye, hoping she had good instincts.

"No, of course not. When you used Lois Evans's security badge I received notification. The system is configured to let me know whenever anyone enters the building after hours. We have valuable technology here that could be dangerous in the wrong hands."

"You mean like yours?"

Andrew dropped Trish's arm and stepped forward, waving the gun at Shelby. "No, not like mine. This technology is revolutionary and has the potential to change life as we know it on this planet. People like you are so shortsighted and ignorant. All you can see is the negative."

"Negative? You mean like seizures? Coma? Death?"

"Statistically acceptable losses. There are always unfortunate losses when it comes to progress. It's how we learn. We make mistakes and we fix them. Don't forget, Ms. Hutchinson, you also signed a release and you ignored your briefing about your trip. You were aware of the risks and made your own choice."

He had her there, but Shelby pressed on. "You're right, Andrew. We fix mistakes, and you made a big one that I am about to fix."

Shelby was happy to see Trish did have good instincts. When Andrew dropped her arm, she had stepped back and cautiously picked up one of the heavy bookends sitting on the table between the two office chairs they had sat in the last time they had faced down Andrew. As Shelby told Andrew how she planned to fix his mistakes, Trish brought the bookend up and swung it at Andrew's head.

Shelby saw the instant the bookend entered Andrew's peripheral vision and she moved. She jumped forward, kicking him into the arc of Trish's swing. The bookend made contact, the gun went off, and Andrew went down in a heap.

Shelby kicked the gun away and stepped over Andrew's prone form to fold Trish into her arms. They sank to the floor, shaking.

You are good, Shelby Hutchinson. Not as good as me, but you are good.

"Thank you," Shelby breathed.

"No, thank you. If you hadn't pissed him off like that, I never would have been able to get to the bookend."

"I guess it's a good thing I'm so annoying then, huh?"

They started to laugh and then to cry, which is how Jake and the police found them a few minutes later when they stormed down the hall and into the office.

While the police busied themselves restraining Andrew and calling for an ambulance and the crime scene team, Jake fell to his knees in front of Shelby and Trish. "You didn't come out, Shel. God, don't ever do this to me again!"

"How did you know we were in trouble? It hadn't been that long, had it? Did you see him come in?"

"No. He must have come in the back. I guess he was a little bit more of a back door kind of guy than you thought."

"Then how did you know, Jake?"

"Trish texted me."

Shelby turned to Trish, who pulled her phone out of her pocket.

"What? You can't text one-handed in your pocket? I've been doing that since high school."

Ah, she is very good, Shelby Hutchinson. Useful and beautiful. You should keep her.

"I plan on it."

"Plan on what?" asked Trish.

"Um, plan on taking you with me the next time I decide to save the world." Shelby winked at Jake.

CHAPTER SIXTEEN

The late April sun was warm on her back. Shelby idly traced patterns through the condensation on her glass. A beautiful day in Berlin, a beautiful woman across the table.

"Is it not dangerous for you to be here again, Shelby Hutchinson?"

"No, Tasha, not this time. It turns out Lois had been working on some modifications to the program to make it safer. She also knew that if I came back here to say good-bye to you, my headaches and seizures would stop too."

"But I thought this Lois was already dead. How can she be helping you?"

Shelby took a sip of her drink. "She is dead, but before she died she made sure her work would be accessible through Head Trip's computers. If Andrew had ever bothered to listen to her, none of this would have happened."

Tasha made a disgusted snort. "Andrew is a greedy capitalist pig. What will happen to him now?"

"He'll go to prison. Head Trip will be closed once they've cleaned up the mess they've made. I think the technology is already technically owned by the military, but Trish is writing about it so none of this will stay secret for long."

Tasha leaned forward and took Shelby's hand. "This is dangerous for you, no? If the government wishes this secret, what will they do to you?"

"It won't be like that, Tasha. This isn't 1985 anymore. Our government isn't like yours."

"Republicans. I will never understand."

Shelby smiled. "It's okay. I just needed to come here again. See you again, to say good-bye. I don't think I'll be taking any more vacations like this one."

Tasha leaned back in her chair, the leather of her jacket squeaking. "It's all right, Shelby Hutchinson. You don't need me anymore. You learned much from me, but now is the time to be yourself."

Shelby laughed. "Yeah, that's me—badass American courier. I'll probably never leave Chicago again."

"Do not be so certain. You are much more badass than you think. You handled Andrew. You are smart and brave and you have a beautiful woman by your side, no?"

Shelby nodded. Trish was indeed by her side. In fact, she was waiting for her at Head Trip, probably holding her hand.

"Yes, Tasha. Trish is with me. I think I have you to thank for that, or I have her to thank for you. Either way, I am grateful to have you both in my life."

Tasha stood and dropped a few deutschmarks on the table. "You only need one of us now. It has been a good ride, Shelby Hutchinson."

Tasha pulled Shelby to her feet and kissed her, leaving her a little breathless. Then Shelby watched as Tasha and her fabulous ass strolled down the block to her bike, climbed on, and rode away.

❖

The room came swimming back into focus. Monitors beeping quietly, soft music in the background, the smell of Trish's perfume, and the warmth of her hand holding tightly to Shelby's. No loud gunshot or the smell of residue. No searing pain in her head or heart-pounding fear. It was finally over.

"Hey there, gorgeous, are you back?"

It was Trish's voice, not Tasha's. That thought was tinged with a little sadness, but seeing the look of concern and love on Trish's face washed the sadness away.

Shelby sat up slowly. "Yeah, I'm back. No head trauma, so it's good, right?"

"I would say that's very good." Trish held Shelby's hand as the technicians removed the monitors and readouts from her head, chest, and arms.

When she was finally free, Shelby slipped to the edge of the bed and stood with some help from Trish.

"You know, I would really like to get out of here. I've had enough of this place to last me several lifetimes and vacations."

"How about we go on a real vacation next time? Some place warm and quiet and painfully dull? No Berlin, no time travel, no spies?"

Shelby hugged Trish. "I can't tell you how good that sounds. But for now, how about lunch? Head Tripping makes me hungry, and I have a real taste for some beer and brats."

"You've got to be kidding!"

Shelby grinned. "Nope, there's a great little German place over on Piedmont. You'll love it."

"Okay, but I am *not* doing the accent, and you can't make me."

"Is fine, Patricia Aronoff. Is just fine."

About the Author

D.L. Line has been many things at different times in her life: a musician, a pharmacy technician, a bartender, a student, a restaurant owner, a marching band director, and a dog sitter, to name a few. Through it all, she has always been a storyteller.

D.L. lives in Virginia with her family, including Snickers the Wonderdog.

D.L. Line's first novel, *On Dangerous Ground*, was recognized by the Alice B. Reader's Selection Committee as a 2010 Lavender Certificate Winner for outstanding debut novel.

Books Available From Bold Strokes Books

Head Trip by D.L. Line. Shelby Hutchinson, a young computer professional, can't wait to take a virtual trip. She soon learns that chasing spies through Cold War Europe might be a great adventure, but nothing is ever as easy as it seems—especially love. (978-160282-187-3)

Desire by Starlight by Radclyffe. The only thing that might possibly save romance author Jenna Hardy from dying of boredom during a summer of forced R&R is a dalliance with Gardiner Davis, the local vet—even if Gard is as unimpressed with Jenna's charms as she appears to be with Jenna's fame. (978-160282-188-0)

River Walker by Cate Culpepper. Grady Wrenn, a cultural anthropologist, and Elena Montalvo, a spiritual healer, must find a way to end the River Walker's murderous vendetta—and overcome a maze of cultural barriers to find each other. (978-160282-189-7)

Blood Sacraments, edited by Todd Gregory. In these tales of the gay vampire, some of today's top erotic writers explore the duality of blood lust coupled with passion and sensuality. (978-1-60282-190-3)

Mesmerized by David-Matthew Barnes. Through her close friendship with Brodie and Lance, Serena Albright learns about the many forms of love and finds comfort for the grief and guilt she feels over the brutal death of her older brother, the victim of a hate crime. (978-1-60282-191-0)

Whatever Gods May Be by Sophia Kell Hagin. Army sniper Jamie Gwynmorgan expects to fight hard for her country and her future. What she never expects is to find love. (978-1-60282-183-5)

nevermore by Nell Stark and Trinity Tam. In this sequel to everafter, Vampire Valentine Darrow and Were Alexa Newland confront a mysterious disease that ravages the shifter population of New York City. (978-1-60282-184-2)

Playing the Player by Lea Santos. Grace Obregon is beautiful, vulnerable, and exactly the kind of woman Madeira Pacias usually avoids, but when Madeira rescues Grace from a traffic accident, escape is impossible. (978-1-60282-185-9)

Midnight Whispers: The Blake Danzig Chronicles by Curtis Christopher Comer. Paranormal investigator Blake Danzig, star of the syndicated show *Haunted California* and owner of Danzig Paranormal Investigations, has been able to see and talk to the dead since he was a small boy, but when he gets too close to a psychotic spirit, all hell breaks loose. (978-1-60282-186-6)

The Long Way Home by Rachel Spangler. They say you can't go home again, but Raine St. James doesn't know why anyone would want to. When she is forced to accept a job in the town she's been publicly bashing for the last decade, she has to face down old hurts and the woman she left behind. (978-1-60282-178-1)

Water Mark by J.M. Redmann. PI Micky Knight's professional and personal lives are torn asunder by Katrina and its aftermath. She needs to solve a murder and recapture the woman she lost—while struggling to simply survive in a world gone mad. (978-1-60282-179-8)

Picture Imperfect by Lea Santos. Young love doesn't always stand the test of time, but Deanne is determined to get her marriage to childhood sweetheart Paloma back on the road to happily ever after, by way of Memory Lane—and Lover's Lane. (978-1-60282-180-4)

The Perfect Family by Kathryn Shay. A mother and her gay son stand hand in hand as the storms of change engulf their perfect family and the life they knew. (978-1-60282-181-1)

Raven Mask by Winter Pennington. Preternatural Private Investigator (and closeted werewolf) Kassandra Lyall needs to solve a murder and protect her Vampire lover Lenorre, Countess Vampire of Oklahoma—all while fending off the advances of the local werewolf alpha female. (978-1-60282-182-8)

The Devil be Damned by Ali Vali. The fourth book in the best-selling Cain Casey Devil series. (978-1-60282-159-0)